SUFFER ME GLADLY

When nurse Sarah Vane's grandmother became ill, Sarah was temporarily flung into turmoil. It wasn't just the distress of seeing her grandmother suffer, but also concern for their future together. But soon Sarah found a job near her grandmother's home and her Gran began to show signs of great recovery. Leaving London and a busy hospital life for the private nursing of a spoilt teenager was bound to be a little tricky but Sarah was sure she could cope. If only she was so sure about coping with Dr Jonathan Lord!

SUFFER ME GLADLY

Jane Weldrick

ATLANTIC LARGE PRINT
Chivers Press, Bath, England.
Curley Publishing, Inc.,
South Yarmouth, Mass., USA.

Library of Congress Cataloging-in-Publication Data

Weldrick, Jane.
   Suffer me gladly / Jane Weldrick.
      p. cm.—(Atlantic large print)
   ISBN 0-7927-0720-6 (softcover)
   1. Large type books. I. Title.
[PR6073.E375S84   1991]
823'.914—dc20   91-12238
                                                                        CIP

British Library Cataloguing in Publication Data available

This Large Print edition is published by Chivers Press, England, and Curley Publishing, Inc, U.S.A. 1991

Published by arrangement with the author's estate

U.K. Hardback ISBN 0 7451 8197 X
U.K. Softback ISBN 0 7451 8209 7
U.S.A. Softback ISBN 0 7927 0720 6

© Jane Weldrick 1982

SUFFER ME GLADLY

CHAPTER ONE

An evening gallop on King Cole always, or nearly always, did wonders for Dr. Jonathan Lord's well-being, both physical and mental.

But that evening, as rider and stallion emerged from the rough land and woods beyond the big pastures owned by his friend Paul Courtney, who also owned King Cole, Jonathan's dark brows were as thunderous as the clouds massing in the eastern sky, his firm mouth set. Tonight, not even King Cole's immense strength and somewhat arrogant personality, perhaps matching his own, pleased him. Nor did they serve to clear his mind of professional problems, which was unusual.

Melissa Courtney, nearly seventeen years old, was the only child of the master of Courtney Place. A nurse was already on her way from London, from dear old St Benedict's, no less, to aid and abet in restoring the girl to health, but this did nothing to improve the doctor's mood. This, in fact, was the cause of his anxiety.

A young nurse ... Dr. Lord grunted as he urged the stallion on. He would be the first to admit that private work for nurses was often necessary, but why would a young Staff Nurse from such an eminent hospital seek private work if not for the absurdly high pay?

His patient was pretty, wilful and thoroughly spoiled by her father, and going through a pretty bad time. She needed nursing discipline, a firm hand, but he doubted if a young girl, however highly recommended, would be able to cope, or even fit in. He rode along the edge of the big ploughed field towards the gate which would take him on to the narrow lane, and thence across the spinney to the big house, deep in thought. The stallion sensed his rider's dark mood, and for once behaved himself impeccably.

★ ★ ★

The northbound train thundered towards York, carrying Sarah Vane away from London for the second time in four days. When she had first travelled home she had been tense and anxious about her grandmother's heart attack, too worried to eat or relax at St. Ben's until she was on the train, still not knowing what she would find when she arrived.

'Angina,' her young brother Michael had told her on the telephone, in the hall of the Nurses' Home. 'They wired her up to a thingummy—' 'Her' being their grandmother Helen Vane, who had cared for brother and sister since their father died a few years earlier, and for the three of them before that ... a small motherless family.

'Of course I'll come,' she had assured Michael. 'Right away. I'll have to see the SNO, but I have a few days due. I'll ring and let you know when to expect me.'

Everyone at St. Ben's had been marvellous. Sarah had been a Staff Nurse at the great old London teaching hospital for two years, and was both liked and respected by the medical and nursing staff. She left on her first rushed journey up north with everyone's good wishes ringing in her ears, helping her to bear the nagging fear of what she would find at home.

By the time Sarah had arrived the first time the crisis was over. Cousin Jean, plump, rosy, the mother of three small boys, had arrived from Whitby and had the housekeeping reins in her capable hands, so that Sarah had been able to devote herself to nursing her grandmother for a few days.

It seemed strange, using her skills at her grandmother's bedside. But more than skill or compassion entered into the nursing. There was love. Sarah had felt a strange chill as she held the fragile wrist in her fingers and watched the rise and fall of the older woman's chest as she lay propped up on high pillows. Only sixty-five, she thought, but tired out. Michael and I should have noticed but he is so young, and I only come home two or three times a year...

The doctor's verdict was cheering. Rest, and more rest. A week or two in bed, and then a gentle recuperation before trying to lead a normal life—a life without gardening or baking bread or papering walls. So Sarah encouraged Helen Vane, assuring her that there was nothing to worry about, explaining the doctor's findings, glad to see her grandmother smiling, the fear leaving her tired face.

At the same time, Sarah realised that she would have to reorganise her life. She would have to find a nursing job nearer home, so that even when her grandmother was fully recovered she would be near at hand, able to come back to the stone cottage when she had time off duty—close enough to bring assurance to the older woman and the lad who was not a boy, nor yet a man.

Since their mother had died at Michael's birth Helen Vane had been their mainstay; and then, later, when their father, Helen's only son, lost his life in a local pot-holing rescue attempt—the leader of the team, strong and fearless, always willing to descend into the labyrinth of tunnels which honeycombed the area—she became mother and father to the girl and boy. Sarah was just starting nursing training at the General and Michael was still at school.

Cousin Jean assured Sarah she would stay for a while, until they were 'sorted out', but they all knew she would have to put her own family first eventually. While caring for the sick woman, Sarah's mind worked frantically. There would be other attacks—not certainly, but probably. She would see the Senior Nursing Officer as soon as she got back to St. Ben's.

That evening, when Sarah and Jean were having supper, and Michael was tucking into sandwiches and coffee over his books in the other room, Jean had suggested that Sarah applied for a post at the Northern General.

'After all, love, you trained there. They'd have you back like a shot, and it's only about fifteen miles away.'

Busy with the dishes, she failed to notice Sarah's sudden flush, followed by a deathly pallor. Sarah stirred her coffee, her head bent, her heart pounding. Only Gran had known what had happened at the General. Michael had been too young to notice or understand ... Jean knew nothing.

She blinked down at the table, fighting back hot tears. No, not the General. Anywhere else! Too many painful memories. Too many people who would still remember.

'Oh, I'll find somewhere, Jean. But I don't fancy the General. Miss Warden, the SNO, might have some ideas, and there are agencies, too.'

'Is she nice, Miss Warden?'

'I suppose so,' Sarah said. 'She's fair and

efficient, and very strict. But human underneath. She must be—'

'Can you picture yourself at her age, running a hospital?' her cousin asked curiously.

Sarah thought. 'Of course,' she said. 'I'm in line for a Sister's job in a year or two—I forgot to tell you. "Sister" ...' Her eyes shone at the idea.

'Not you,' said Jean cheerfully. 'You'll get married and have kids!'

That's what they all say, Sarah had thought, as she stacked the plates. But marriage was for others ... something the young nurses talked about endlessly—boys, engagement rings, honeymoons. But to Sarah it seemed unreal, hollow, not for her. Wonderful when she was nineteen and foolish. But falling in love hurt too much, and she did not intend to risk it again, ever.

* * *

Sarah opened her eyes. South Yorkshire—slag-heaps and tips of chemical waste, tall black chimneys, bleak mills and warehouses.

She took out the neat dark-blue folder, labelled: 'St. Benedict's Hospital, London, E.9. Highly Confidential', and glanced at the neatly-typed pages and charts. 'Melissa Courtney, age sixteen, home address Courtney Place, near Shepley, Yorkshire—

next-of-kin, Paul Courtney, father—' and the SNO's voice drifted into her mind, saying: 'A bad patient, I understand, Staff Nurse—'

For a while Sarah studied the notes given into her professional safe-keeping on a temporary basis, and then she put them away. She ran a comb through her hair, glad that the carriage was almost empty, and put on fresh lipstick, noting professionally that her face was too pale, with faint blue shadows under her eyes. She slipped into her shabby sheepskin coat and checked her belongings and then sat relaxed, watching the shadows of the trees, long and narrow along the ground.

Another twenty minutes and she would be at the station. What would private nursing be like? After all those years, well, nearly six years, it would be strange. She was not worried about her ability, just the contrast between working in a private house after the vast organisation of the hospital.

On the other hand, she told herself, you'll be free. Free to go home to the cottage as soon as you come off-duty, if you hurry; free to go there on every day off, always in close touch with the family.

Perhaps there was a catch in it. There must be, for there always was! What, she mused, would be the snag? Her new patient ... Melissa Courtney?

Sarah grinned, and gave the briefcase holding the offending folder a flick with her fingernail. Surely Staff Nurse Sarah Vane could handle one spoiled teenage girl. And Miss Warden had said that Melissa's father was a sensible man, as well as charming. And when Miss Warden deemed someone to be sensible, you could be certain of it.

Now the ancient pile of York Minster appeared on the skyline to the east, and the train began its long deceleration into the station. Sarah sighed with pleasure and descended on to the platform, her ticket, first class by courtesy of her new employer, ready for the collector at the barrier. The light was fading fast and a bitter wind blew through the station. Four days age she had run for the local train to Nortondale, but the journey today would end by road.

'For Courtney Place, miss?' a rough country voice asked her.

Sarah turned and smiled at the short, broad man who put out his hand for her luggage. He was a true countryman, red of face, blue-eyed, in a rough tweed jacket and shapeless trousers, heavy boots on his feet. He led the way through the parking area to where a well-used station-wagon waited, and introduced himself as Tom Sanders.

'And you'll be Miss Vane,' he went on, his voice deep, the long vowel sound of her surname flattened and drawn out in the way Sarah knew so well.

'Yes, that's right,' she replied as she

climbed into the passenger seat and Tom settled himself behind the wheel.

'You'll be feeling the cold,' he told her politely as he drove out on to the road, and Sarah huddled down into her sheepskin and said that she was fine, feeling no need to tell him yet that she was as Yorkshire as he was, and not given to feeling the cold, or minding a bit of rain, or any such nonsense. There would be time for such intimacies later, when she had become part of the Courtney household.

As he drove, Tom told Sarah that he looked after the cars and stables, and gave the 'master' only he said 'mester'—a hand around the place.

'Aye. Engines and 'osses,' he said, switching on the headlamps as they sped along the main road. 'But 'osses, mainly.'

Of course. Horses. Sarah realised she had been acutely aware that the man beside her smelled of something familiar. She had always loved horses, and her father had taught her to ride as a little girl.

She grinned to herself and wondered if she would be able to ride. It would be rather a delicate matter, really, because of Melissa's accident. And of course her patient would certainly not be riding for a long time, if ever, which left just her employer and Tom, unless there was a Mrs. Courtney who rode, too. Strange that there had been no mention of

Paul Courtney's wife ... Melissa's mother. Perhaps, Sarah thought compassionately, they were widower father and motherless child.

She half listened as Tom rambled on about the horses, watching the darkening fields, thinking about her new young patient with the multiple fractures and spoiled nature, and wondering how her grandmother was.

She felt sure that Gran was going to make a good recovery and that the new job would be interesting, if a little unusual. The new salary would make all the difference—enabling her to bridge the gap between stinting and scraping to make things easier at home, and knowing that all was well.

After all, what could go wrong?'

It was at that moment Sarah saw the horse and its rider—the big black stallion, looming out of the shadow of the dark hedgerow, silhouetted against the last light of the evening sky. She stared through the station-wagon windscreen, and it was as if her eyes met those of the man who rode the horse, although in fact he was just a dark shape, wide-shouldered and still.

Tom Sanders brought the station-wagon to a halt and opened his door. Muttering something to her, he clambered out and she saw him touch his cap to the man on the horse, who dismounted easily and looped the reins over a gatepost.

'Good evening, Tom,' she heard him say, in a quiet, very deep voice, and she knew that she was staring at him rudely through Tom's open window. Was this Paul Courtney? This man certainly had an air of power and authority, with his physical presence and his extraordinary stillness. He was tall and powerfully built, dressed, as far as Sarah could see, in a heavy jacket or anorak, dark polo sweater and cord trousers. She felt a slight but unmistakable sense of chill and knew at once that she would rather not work for this man . . . that his mere presence in the dark country lane in some way diminished her own personality.

Tom led the man towards the vehicle.

'I've been to the station to fetch Miss Vane,' he said. 'This be Dr. Lord, miss.'

The black stallion moved restlessly, blowing down his nostrils; the cold night air ruffled Sarah's hair, and the man stooped and put his big hand through the window, bestowing upon her a smile that did not reach his dark eyes.

'Welcome to Courtney Place,' he said.

Sarah withdrew her cold hand from the warm and powerful grip, and reluctantly admitted to herself that it was a good doctor's hand, big and long-fingered, strong and sensitive. She was in a hurry to terminate the physical contact, however, and said the first thing that came into her mind.

11

'I didn't know people rode in the dark.' Her voice sounded uncertain and rather foolish, and for a long moment the dark eyes regarded her curiously, as if she were a small child.

'They don't. But this horse is a unique animal and actually likes it. He needs the exercise, so I took him out.'

'I see,' Sarah said meekly. Tom was beside the horse, holding its bridle and talking to it.

'I expect you'll be glad to get to the house after your train journey and this drive.'

She was silent, made nervous by the careful scrutiny she was receiving in the dim light from the dashboard.

'Night-duty, perhaps?' Dr. Lord suggested, his voice implying that she looked tired, and she began to feel put out. All right, so it had been a difficult few days, with a lot of tearing about, and nursing her grandmother for long stretches.

'No. Just a busy time,' she said. It was a temptation to give a brief résumé of her situation, but something stopped her. She did not want this man's sympathy—nor did she feel any need to reveal herself. Later, perhaps, but she was not certain.

'I understand you're in charge of Melissa Courtney,' she said, anxious to be on their way again with Tom Sanders at the wheel. 'My SNO at St. Benedict's told me a little about you. She's let me bring a copy of

Melissa's case notes, on loan. I've been looking at them on the train.'

'I know Miss Warden,' Dr. Lord said, as Tom climbed back into the station-wagon. 'She speaks very well of your work, Staff.'

'Even though I look tired and unsuitable for the job?' Sarah regretted the words as she spoke, but it was too late. She bit her lip, and would have apologised, but he gave her no chance.

'Some food and an early night are prescribed,' he said quietly, and gave a small formal bow and turned towards the stallion. Tom let in the clutch and they headed into the gathering dusk.

'He's a lovely horse,' Sarah said.

'Oh, aye, miss. Only the mester and the doctor ride him—he's a man's 'orse, I reckon.

Sarah smiled, feeling her temper subside.

'Dr. Lord rides well, then?'

'Aye, he does that. A real handful, yon!'

Sarah concealed a sudden delighted grin. Who was the real handful, then? The black stallion or the dark, ironic doctor? Or were they both?

Tom told her they would be at Courtney Place in about fifteeen minutes by road, whereas the doctor on horseback would cut across the land and have King Cole back in his stable and be gone by then.

Sarah turned up her coat collar and retreated into her thoughts, her mind returning to St. Ben's and her departure...

She recalled how kind the SNO had been—a small, cool woman who had spent most of her nursing life at the hospital. Respected, if not loved, by all for her sense of justice and her dedication to nursing.

Responding to the older woman's skilful questions, Sarah had related the whole story. The SNO asked about Michael's plans, and then came straight to the point.

'I am prepared to let you go immediately, Staff Nurse,' she said, regarding Sarah across her tidy desk. 'A worried nurse is no use to me. You must find a post near your home.'

Sarah nodded. 'Yes, Miss Warden, but—'

The older woman picked up a letter and smiled at Sarah.

'I think I may be able to help you. By a strange coincidence, there is a private post available in your part of the world. Nortondale, is it not? I believe Courtney, near Shepley, is not far away?'

Sarah frowned. 'It's quite near, Miss Warden.'

The SNO nodded. 'Good. If you should decide to take this post, Staff Nurse, I would like you to know that you will be sadly missed here, and that there will always be an opening for you at St. Benedict's.'

Sarah felt tears stinging her eyes, and she swallowed hard, and looked down at her white starched lap.

'You were destined to become one of our youngest Sisters,' the SNO went on. 'I hope you will return.'

Sarah nodded, speechless.

'Now, let me see. I felt so confident about this opening I took it upon myself to accept for you, provisionally. But of course—'

Sarah waited. A job near home, so soon, and so easily? It was too good to be true. But not at the Northern General, not there, please ... But no, the SNO had said a private post, hadn't she?

'—Melissa Courtney,' Miss Warden went on. 'She was admitted here a few weeks ago, with fractures and concussion. Discharged the day before yesterday, on the condition she was nursed at home. Her father is extremely well-off.'

'I remember the case,' Sarah said slowly. 'I was in Casualty at the time.'

Prompted by the SNO Sarah went on to show her unusual memory for facts. A riding accident while taking a jump at Olympia—a girl of sixteen, brought in unconscious. She frowned as she recalled seeing the slender figure barely lifting the outline of the red blanket on the stretcher. The mass of tangled chestnut curls and the waxen face, with immense blue eyes which opened and stared up at her, deeply in shock. Sarah recalled walking beside the stretcher trolley to X-ray, gently holding the girl's chin with one hand, looking down and telling her she would be all right, although she probably did not hear.

She met Miss Warden's eyes, for once unguarded and amused, and smiled involuntarily. Who would ever forget the dreaded Melissa, who made life on the private ward a misery for the younger nurses with her sulks and tantrums? It was a talking point at meal times...

'Potts and scaphoid,' Sarah said simply. 'Concussion, at first suspected sub-dural. Severe bruising and shock.'

Miss Warden put down her pen and smiled.

'Well done, Staff Nurse, considering you did not nurse her. Now, to cut a long story short, the patient was obviously unhappy here, and Mr. Coutts allowed her to be taken home, by special ambulance, of course. She has her leg and wrist in plaster still, and for some time to come, and can expect severe headaches—'

She paused, and Sarah boldly supplied: 'Without the relief of analgesics, because of the concussion—'

'Correct, Staff Nurse. Miss Courtney was a bad patient. Difficult, I would say. Possibly a rich man's spoilt daughter. The salary is extremely generous, which you can use, I understand.' She smiled dryly. 'And Mr. Courtney seems to me to be an ideal employer. He is kindly and pleasant, and devoted to his daughter. But not foolish, just devoted. I did not hear him mention his wife, so perhaps the child has no mother—'

Sarah sat lost in thought. She would have been a fool to turn it down. It was all there, waiting for her, the answers to her problems.

'Shall I ring Mr. Courtney and tell him about you?'

Sarah nodded. 'Please, yes! Yes, I accept the post. And thank you, Miss Warden.'

* * *

'Nearly there,' Tom Sanders remarked, and Sarah peered through the windscreen into the darkness.

The thought of a warm fire, a hot drink, a hot bath and change of clothes appealed strongly, and she smiled to herself, and told herself that she was a fool to let her first glimpse of the GP upset her—even though he had caught her with her defences down, back-chatting to him like a silly teenager.

After all, she would see him every day, and it was inconceivable that she should react to him like an eighteen-year-old student nurse at the mercy of a cocksure young medical student, all blushes and shaking hands. Hate at first sight was absurd and out of the question anyway, for she had a job to do, was a bright and mature twenty-four, and quite used to arrogant medicos.

But, a small voice asked her, why then was it that Dr. Lord made her feel so uncertain of herself, so anxious yet reluctant to explain herself, so very un-Sarah-ish?

His face came into her mind, the mocking dark eyes, heavy-lidded, missing nothing; the powerful, athletic build, the mocking smile on the long mobile mouth; the thick dark hair falling across his wide brow, outlining the strong structure of cheekbone and jaw. Oh, sure, it was a clever and immensely attractive face, with a voice to match...

Sarah shook her head, narrowing her eyes. Okay, so Jonathan Lord was another attractive doctor. Well, he wasn't the first in her life. She had met many, and loved one, once, way back. But the others afterwards, at St. Ben's, had been unlucky and got nowhere for all their persuasive charms.

Only Philip Gresham, junior Surgical Registrar at the Northern General had succeeded, when he broke her heart, six years ago. And since then Sarah had had many casual men friends, all held at arm's length, all treated alike. Life in London had been pleasant, if not exactly pulsating, which was the way she wanted it.

Sarah had never told anyone that sometimes she ached to have someone of her own to love and care for, a home and children. By the time the pain had gone away completely it might be too late, but until it did, she preferred to present a cold front to the world of love and romance.

Tom Sanders was blowing his horn. A shadowy figure emerged from the small lodge by the great iron gates and opened them, waving them through with shouted greetings, lost in the vehicle's noise and the wind. At the end of the long, curving drive Sarah saw the house which was to be her home temporarily.

A tall man stood silhouetted against the open front door, and Sarah guessed that the lodge-keeper had telephoned to announce her arrival. She found herself shaking hands with Paul Courtney, erect and thin, with greying hair and tired blue eyes, and being led into a room where logs blazed in an enormous grate.

She took a beautiful crystal glass of sherry and let her employer push forward a big leather armchair towards the blaze.

Sarah thought that Paul Courtney made a perfect picture of a gentleman farmer, in his old but impeccably cut tweed suit, his old-school tie and highly polished brown brogues. His warm smile and quiet voice dispelled her slight nervousness, and his concern for her well-being was absolutely genuine.

'I understand you have a small domestic—or perhaps I should say family—crisis on your hands,' he remarked. 'I am glad, Miss Vane, that it has occurred when I—we ... so badly need someone. My daughter—but you will know of the case, if you're from St. Benedict's.'

'Of course,' Sarah replied, liking this tall, friendly man. 'Yes, Mr. Courtney, I badly needed to find a post away from London—here in the north, in fact. I feel I've been very lucky. It's a lovely house—'

Paul Courtney nodded. 'Yes, it is, and I want you to be happy here. I wouldn't dream of prying into your private affairs, of course. But it's a relief, now that you're here. Dr. Lord's partner's aunt, a retired nurse, has been lending us a hand with Melissa since she arrived two days ago. Now that we've met I'm sure she'll be in very good hands.'

Sarah smiled politely, feeling she would have been quite happy to tell her employer the reason why she left St. Ben's, but that it was not essential. One day, perhaps, when she knew him better.

For a few minutes Paul Courtney made polite and impersonal conversation, putting Sarah at her ease. He made no attempt to ask her any searching questions about her qualifications or special skills, appearing to take them for granted. He spoke of his daughter and her injuries, a look of deep affection on his thin face, and then paused as a small plump woman of about sixty entered.

'This is Mrs. Ruddy, our housekeeper. She used to be Melissa's Nanny—'

'And I still am, I reckon—how do you do,

Nurse?' said Mrs. Ruddy, and Sarah held out her hand, liking the older woman at first sight.

'Staff Nurse—' Paul Courtney corrected Mrs. Ruddy gently. 'Staff Nurse Vane.'

Sarah laughed. 'Oh, "Nurse" will do, Mrs. Ruddy. "Staff Nurse" is such a mouthful! I'm not at the hospital now.'

The housekekeper shot her a grateful look and said that would be grand, and retreated, telling Sarah that she could have her supper in her room if and when she wanted it, which she must do, after all that travelling, for she must be clemmed.

Sarah grinned at the old north-country word, and said that she was, which surprised both of them, her employer and his older employee.

Paul Courtney suggested that they should take a look at the patient, before Sarah had an early night. Evelyn, who must be the retired nurse, would be on call during the first night, if Melissa should want anything.

'It's not that the lass is ill, as you know,' he told her, leading the way across the entrance hall, and through a heavy door into what was obviously an extension of the main building. 'But she can't move about much, get to the bathroom and so on, without a bit of help and sometimes her head hurts, so someone has to be on hand—'

Sarah murmured that she understood, and

that she was sure that she and 'Evelyn' would be able to work out their spells of night-duty perfectly well.

'Mrs. Ruddy takes her turn, as well,' Paul went on thoughtfully, preceding her along a thickly-carpeted corridor. 'And I do, so you won't have to worry about losing your sleep.'

He opened a door and entered the big, airy room, lit only by a small lamp beside the high hospital bed. Sarah could see at a glance that no expense or trouble had been spared to make the room one in which a patient would be comfortable and pampered. The colour scheme was white and apricot, echoed by the sleeveless nightdress the slender, sleeping girl wore, her small face white against the pastel pillow, her long mass of lack-lustre hair tied back with a ribbon.

The small fair woman seated by the bed rose and faced her visitors.

'Ah, good evening, Evelyn,' Paul Courtney said. 'I want you to meet Miss Vane—Staff Nurse Vane.'

He completed the introductions, but Sarah barely heard, so strong was the first impact of the room, her patient and the older nurse on her. She took the outstretched hand in hers, smiling—a small, cool, firm hand which removed itself after the briefest contact—and met the gaze of coolly searching blue eyes in a pale, intelligent face.

'I've made full reports for you to read,' the

small fair woman said. 'She has a certain amount of discomfort—she hates the plasters, and is quite badly bruised. Headaches, of course—but she's coming on ... slowly.'

Sarah nodded, and arranged to see her relief nurse early the next morning. She said good night—slightly embarrassed that she had not caught the other nurse's name, but able to cover her social error by saying: 'Thank you, Sister,' as she left the room. How useful titles could be, on occasion, when at a loss for a name.

Mrs. Ruddy was hovering in the big hall, obviously wanting to escort Sarah to her room, and Paul Courtney paused, his hand on the massive carved post at the foot of the great staircase.

'Come to me if there is anything you need,' he said quietly. 'I love my daughter, Staff Nurse. She's a difficult lass, sometimes, but—' he paused and frowned—'I want her to get better soon.'

'She will, Mr. Courtney,' Sarah said quickly. 'It's just a matter of time. Young people recuperate very fast—you'll be surprised.'

The man smiled. 'Yes, I'm sure you're right. Mrs. Ruddy will look after you—and by the way, there's a small car you can use—Tom will have it ready for you whenever you need it.'

A lump came into Sarah's throat, and she

tried to speak calmly. 'Oh, that's very kind—I—thank you, thanks very much.'

Paul Courtney smiled again and said 'sleep well,' as he watched Sarah climb the staircase.

Sarah ascertained what time Sister Evelyn left in the morning, and told Mrs. Ruddy she wanted to be downstairs well before that.

'Of course, love—I mean "nurse",' Mrs. Ruddy replied, leading the way into the bedroom.

It was a big room, low-ceilinged, with simple walnut furnishings and soft green carpet, and velvet curtains at the casement windows.

And flowers. Someone had taken the trouble to fill the room with bowls of out-of-season flowers which filled the warm air with their fragrance.

The housekeeper smiled at the surprise on Sarah's face.

'That was Melissa, the lamb,' she confided. 'Insisted, she did. Said all nurses like flowers, and Tom went all the way to town to fetch them, after she'd done telephoning the order.'

'That was sweet of her,' Sarah said, bending to inhale the scent of the delicate, long-stemmed rosebuds in their cut-glass bowl. 'Is she always doing things like that?'

The older woman made a comical grimace. 'Who? My Miss Melissa? No, she isn't, and that's a fact, but she has some nice little ways sometimes.'

When Sarah had washed her hands and face in the adjoining white and pink bathroom, she returned to where a laden tray stood on a small table, and the housekeeper had drawn up a comfortable chair in green brocade.

'Sit down, now, and have your soup,' she said. 'Home-made today.' She lifted the lid from the miniature brown earthenware casserole, and a delicious aroma rose with the steam. 'See, some wholemeal bread an' all. An' you can manage this bit o' chicken breast, and a slice of my apple pie, I'm sure. Margaret—she's the maid—will bring you tea or coffee when you ring.'

Mrs. Ruddy stood and watched as her new charge ate hungrily, a smile of content on her round face under the crown of silver hair.

'The doctor'll be along tomorrow,' she remarked.

'Fine. I met him on the way from the station. Tom Sanders spoke to him, and we had a few words. He was riding a big black horse.'

Mrs. Ruddy nodded. 'Aye, that'll have been King Cole. Beats me how he can dare to go near that beast, let alone ride him. Just to look at him is enough for the likes of me. They're all horse-mad round here. The master, the doctor, and of course Melissa wouldn't be as she is, poor lamb, if it weren't for pony riding—'

Sarah looked suitably sympathetic. It seemed that Mrs. Ruddy didn't hold with a lot of horse riding. And no wonder, with her 'precious lamb' so badly injured.

'She keeps house for both of 'em,' Mrs. Ruddy offered.

'She? Oh, I see—you mean Sister er—I'm afraid I didn't catch her name, downstairs,' Sarah said.

Mrs. Ruddy was again in full spate. 'Aye. They say she's a good cook, yon. For a nurse, like. Doesn't do much nursing these days, now she's getting on a bit. It was her nephew, Dr. Lord's partner, young fellow he is, who thought of her coming to see Melissa 'til you got here. And to stop and lend you a hand, I'm hoping.'

Sarah put down her knife and fork and shook her head at the apple pie.

'Just a tiny piece,' she said, cutting a narrow slice. 'And who is the doctor's partner, Mrs. Ruddy?'

Not that it was important, but as long as the housekeeper stood there she had to find something to say. It would be rude to eat in total silence.

'Dr. Gresham, of course. They call him Philip, mostly. Nice young chap.'

Mrs. Ruddy was busy turning down the bedspread, her broad back towards Sarah, and therefore could not see the blood drain from Sarah's face, leaving it chalky white, her eyes suddenly wide and dark.

Of course. Paul Courtney had said 'Miss Gresham' at Melissa's bedside, but her ears and her mind had failed to register it, absorbed as she was in her new, sleeping patient, and the general atmosphere of the big house, and the sick-room itself.

So Philip was here!

Sarah's heart was beating erratically, and she sat and tried to breathe slowly, to regain control, afraid that her shocked reaction might show.

This, then, was the price she must pay. The snag she had jokingly wondered about when she learned of her good fortune in finding such a post so easily.

'Everything all right?' Mrs. Ruddy was asking. 'Shall I get you some tea or suchlike? You look fair worn out, child.'

'Please,' Sarah said, trying hard to smile and relax. Anything to get the kindly creature out of the room, so that she could pull herself together, be alone with her reeling thoughts. She recalled that Philip had spoken of his aunt once or twice—an ex-army nurse working somewhere abroad ... good old Aunt Evelyn.

The plump, smiling young maid brought coffee and put it on the table and withdrew. Sarah got up and drew the heavy curtains against the dark, windy night. It was too dark to see anything outside. Neither could she see into her own mind. Her thoughts were dark and confused and totally chaotic.

To learn that Philip Gresham was near by, a partner of Dr. Lord's, was a hideous stroke of fate, when she had thought herself free of those painful memories of a time she had been so foolish and vulnerable.

But now, it seemed, there was to be no escape.

CHAPTER TWO

The pale winter sunlight poured into the oak-panelled dining-room as Sarah breakfasted alone, studying Sister Gresham's reports on Melissa, and thinking about her patient.

Already she had telephoned her grandmother and given a brief but enthusiastic account of her new post, saying that she would write soon and describe everything in full.

When she first came downstairs quite early she went straight to Melissa's room and took the night report, and for the first time met her patient as a silent, unsmiling but very wakeful girl.

For a few minutes the two nurses talked about their charge and arranged duties for the coming week. Sarah stood by the bedside and spoke to her patient, who made no reply but stared down at her breakfast with a faint look of distaste on her small white face. Sarah noticed that she had a shabby old red robe pulled round her shoulders, although a pretty blue bed-jacket hung over the back of a chair near by, but she decided that the girl was best left to get on with her unloved breakfast in peace. She just contented herself with saying her name, and that she was from St. Benedict's, and was rewarded with a long, cold stare, and the words, in a small, very well-bred voice: 'Oh, that place.'

As Sarah ate she pondered on Melissa Courtney's obvious depression, the shabby dressing-gown hugged closely around her over the thin, very school-girlish nightdress, for Melissa was going on for seventeen, an age when girls were interested in pretty things, fastidious about their clothes. There was a lot to do, she decided, and it wasn't all going to be routine nursing. This was a sick, unhappy girl who would demand a high degree of professional skill and patience, and not just for her physical injuries . . .

As Sarah made her way back to the sick-room she passed Margaret carrying the tray, and she took a good look at it, sad to see the poached egg and toast untouched, and just half a slice of toast missing from the little silver rack. The maid made a rueful face and said that every meal was the same, and Sarah nodded and went towards the battlefield, her face wearing a kindly smile.

Melissa sat in an armchair looking out of the window, wrapped in the skimpy old gown, her hair tangled on her shoulders.

'So you got out all right?' Sarah said. 'Did Margaret help you?' Her reply was a brief nod.

'Fine,' said. 'Now, would you like me to give you a wash?'

Silence. Sarah patiently repeated herself.

Melissa frowned and turned from her contemplation of the morning sky. 'Miss Gresham brought me a bowl when I first woke, thank you.'

Sarah smiled even more. 'Of course. But I mean a proper wash all over, in your smashing bathroom. I'll sit you on the chair and take it slowly, a bit at a time. It'll make you feel a lot better.'

Melissa considered. 'They used to wash me all over in bed, at the hospital. I hated it.' She turned the full force of her blue gaze on Sarah who busied herself tidying the bed that Margaret had made, after a fashion.

'Most people hate bed baths,' Sarah offered. One of the reasons she wanted to wash Melissa was that it would help to pass the time, for the days must seem very long to this highly-strung youngster, hardly able to walk, even with crutches, with the use of only one hand and liable to develop shattering headaches at any time, without recourse to pain-killing drugs, which were not permitted so soon after concussion.

Melissa gave one of her shrugs, to which Sarah was to become thoroughly accustomed as the days and weeks passed at Courtney Place. But now they were irritating, although Sarah was too good a nurse to let them worry her.

She decided to try another tack. 'Before long they'll take your plaster off and give you a smaller one that you can walk on. Won't that be good?'

Melissa shrugged. 'I suppose so.'

'What can you do on your one crutch? It's very difficult, with one hand, isn't it?'

'Not much,' was the grudging reply. 'A few steps. I've got a wheel chair—'

'Oh, fine,' Sarah said, but was rewarded with a frozen stare. 'Don't you like it?'

'Being pushed? No, thanks!'

Oh, heavens, Sarah thought, the poor, poor lass! There must be some way to get through to her, but it obviously was not by talking about her injuries.

'Mrs. Ruddy can tidy round in here while I wash you, or rather while I help you to wash,' she said quietly. 'I might even shampoo your hair, later.'

Melissa frowned. 'Shampoo my hair?'

'Yes.'

'How?'

'We have ways of making you beautiful,' Sarah grinned. 'Jugs and bowls in the bathroom, with Mrs. Ruddy or Margaret to help. You'd be surprised.'

'Don't bother,' Melissa said, looking out of the window, her small face set.

'No bother at all—you've such pretty hair,' Sarah said, and to her surprise Melissa consented to hobble to the bathroom, where she was expertly wrapped in warm fluffy towels and washed from face to toes. Sarah made no comment on the extensive bruising on temple, shoulder, arm, side and hip, still purple but beginning to turn brown and yellow, but was deft and gentle in her ministrations. She let the girl use her good hand as much as possible, all the time chatting about this and that, recalling amusing incidents in the casualty ward concerning children, now and then rewarded by a faint smile on Melissa's pretty mouth.

Leaving her patient sitting wrapped in a towelling robe, Sarah put her head round the bathroom door and asked Margaret, who was mopping the bedroom floor, for a clean nightdress, miming silently the words: 'A pretty one, and a decent housecoat,' to which the little maid responded with obvious delight, rummaging in the cupboards and coming over with her arms laden with pale green and delicate cream.

'Here we go,' Sarah said, slipping the pale

green frothy nightdress over Melissa's head.

'I don't want this one,' a muffled voice said as the towel dropped to the floor.

'Too late now, and it's very pretty,' said Sarah.

'And I don't want this,' to the elegant cream cord housecoat, and Melissa sat herself down and sulked. 'Where's my red dressing-gown?'

'It's here,' Sarah pointed out, stirring the bedraggled red heap on the floor beside the towel. 'It's too small for you, love—'

'I had it when I first went away to school,' the girl muttered.

'Look, I understand,' Sarah said. 'We all have weird old things we hang on to. But your Dad is paying me to do a job, and you're making it hard for me.'

'In what way?'

'Well, it's my job to make you clean and pretty, as well as nursing you. What do I tell him when he sees you looking like a—'

'Like a what?'

'Oh, I don't know—like a daft girl who doesn't know how attractive she is?'

'Me attractive?'

Sarah pursed her lips. She would win this one if it took all day...

'Yes, fairly. But not in that thing.' She stirred the red bundle with her foot. 'Anyway, it smells.'

Melissa had the grace to look horrified.

'Smells?'
'Sure.'
'What of?'
'Old red dressing-gown. What else?'

Suddenly the small pale face fell apart into a wide smile, and Sarah heard her patient laugh. It was a small victory.

Sarah held out the cream robe. 'Here, give me your scaphoid—' She steered the plastered thumb and wrist carefully into the wide sleeve, then the good one, did up the buttons and tied the sash.

In silence they went back to the bedroom and Sarah put the girl back into the armchair.

'Now then, where's your brush and comb? When I've sorted this mop out you can do your exercises for me.'

She ignored the mutinous grimace the girl made and brushed the heavy hair as gently as she could, to avoid damage to the bruised face and scalp.

'I know the local physiotherapist will have taught you some, and they're very important, Melissa, to keep your muscles toned up, and the circulation going in your hand and foot. I'm sure Sister Gresham has been seeing that you do them—just let me find a piece of ribbon for your hair, and you'll do them like a good girl, won't you?'

'Yes to all that,' a deep voice said, and Sarah swung round, knowing that the colour was rising to her cheeks, as Jonathan Lord walked in.

'Good morning, Staff Nurse,' he said coolly and professionally, and Sarah returned the greeting and quickly tied Melissa's hair back and retreated to where the case notes and various reports were neatly laid on a small table.

The doctor spoke to Melissa, touching the pale face with his finger, and took up the reports, asking Sarah a few searching questions, and she gave him her report in the normal hospital manner. His face and voice revealed none of the irony of their first meeting and also no particular warmth or interest, and it could have been any doctor's round at St. Ben's, except for the luxury of their surroundings.

Jonathan asked his young patient a few questions of a somewhat less probing nature, bringing a faint colour to her cheeks, a smile to her mouth, while Sarah stood near by, slender and straight in her neat white dress, dark hair drawn back from her absorbed face as she concentrated.

'Are you eating?' he asked, and Melissa gave her favourite shrug, and he frowned and turned his dark eyes on Sarah.

'Not her breakfast, Doctor,' she replied, giving the young patient a gentle, reproving smile but failing to win a response.

The doctor pondered. 'Fresh air. I want her outside, in the wheel chair. I don't care who pushes it.'

Melissa pouted. 'I don't like it.'

'You need to get out,' he said quietly. 'It will give you an appetite, and if we can get you eating the battle will be over.'

Melissa stared up at him. 'What battle?'

'The battle to get you well. You have lost weight and you have to regain it. Sitting in this room refusing your food won't help. Look, Melissa, we'll have an X-ray done quite soon, and a walking plaster on as quickly as we can. Okay?'

After some more chat, and having refused to take coffee with his patient, Dr. Lord moved away, indicating that he wanted a quiet word with the nurse.

Telling Melissa she would be back to have coffee with her, Sarah followed him dutifully into the corridor.

Without haste he outlined his instructions and Sarah listened carefully and made one or two notes. He would be sending Melissa some mixture to help with her appetite, and he only wished he could give her something for her temper, he added dryly.

Sarah smiled. 'Yes, well, she isn't an easy girl. But I'll manage, Doctor. I've a lot of patience—'

He raised his dark brows again. 'You have? You're very young, Staff.'

Sarah bit her lip and pushed back a strand of hair from her temple. 'Young? Not all that young, Doctor. Do you have something against youth or young nurses?' As she spoke she regretted it, knowing she should have saved the question for another time, later, when, perhaps, she knew the doctor better—if she ever did . . . But the tone of his voice got under her skin.

'Certainly not,' he told her mildly. 'Youth is wonderful, although it's not everything in this profession of healing.'

He searched her face for a reaction to this gentle pronouncement, but Sarah kept calm, outwardly.

'No, Staff Nurse.' His deep voice was gentle, and Sarah felt ashamed of the irritation he caused her, for his manner was perfectly ethical. 'It's just that I prefer to see young nurses like yourself working in hospitals and clinics. That is where you're needed—' he grinned suddenly, his dark face lighting up—'especially with a recommendation like you have from Miss Warden . . . and "a lot of patience". Such a good Staff Nurse is, well, not exactly wasted on a case like this, but—' he shrugged expressively—'you will know what I mean.'

Sarah stared down at her feet and nodded slightly, her soft mouth set. The man was entitled to this viewpoint, which she knew was quite commonly held by doctors. She must not allow herself to be irritated, for they had to work together.

'You may well be right, Doctor. I was quite well thought of at St. Ben's, but—' She broke off, realising she had no intention of doing any explaining at this juncture, to Dr. Lord.

'And at the Northern General, I understand,' he put in quietly, and Sarah caught her breath.

'Oh, yes, I loved it there. But I'm here now, Doctor. I think Mr. Courtney trusts me, and I really intend to get Melissa well.'

He studied her face carefully.

'Yes, of course. And I've no doubt that you will. We will work together very well.' And he was gone.

'He's not bad, Jonathan, is he?' Melissa commented as they drank coffee and looked at the morning paper.

Sarah frowned and pretended to consider.

'No, not bad at all,' she offered, although she was still inwardly raging. He's insufferable, she had told herself as she returned to her patient, but knowing that it was the doctor's manner that annoyed her, not his words. He had merely put into words the view she knew many doctors and nurses held, that private nursing was for those who were 'in it just for the money' and she grudgingly admired his nerve in making his views plain to her so early on in their professional relationship. No, it was the way he smiled, the way he looked right through into her thoughts, that riled her.

And that was not all. How had he found out where she did her training? And what had his junior partner, Philip Gresham, told him about her?

The rest of the morning passed swiftly. Sarah manicured her patient's small pink finger- and toe-nails and said she would look for a pretty pale varnish for them. To her surprise Melissa did her exercises, according to the teachings of the local hospital physiotherapist, a certain Miss Ludvika, or Karen, who it appeared had visited her twice already.

'That's an interesting name,' Sarah commented idly, watching Melissa move her toes up and down.

'Scandinavian. She's very pretty. She went out to dinner with Jonathan—' the girl said. 'Shall we play some records till lunch, Sarah?' And Sarah put on records and wondered if Miss Karen Ludvika was a dazzling, blue-eyed, silver-gilt blonde with the usual lithe and lissom figure of a typical physiotherapist—and disliked Jonathan Lord even more, which puzzled her.

★ ★ ★

Sarah watched her patient as the lovely voice rose and fell at the end of the Russian song.

'You like her, don't you, Melissa?'

Melissa Courtney fell silent for a moment,

frowning, the thin fingers of her good hand stroking the record sleeve lying on the bedspread beside her armchair.

'Very much. Don't you?' The girl bit her lip and turned away.

'She's wonderful. She was at the Albert Hall quite recently,' Sarah said. 'I couldn't get a ticket, though.'

Melissa stared at the photograph on the sleeve, the vivid features and tumbling red hair of the singer, tracing the name, 'June Dennis'—and suddenly Sarah knew that her patient was starting one of the pounding agonising headaches that beset patients recovering from severe concussion, for which pain no analgesics are permitted ... just rest. She could tell, from the muscles tightening round cheeks and mouth, the increased pallor, the shadows under the eyes.

She drew the curtains and removed the records from the bed, persuading Melissa to lie down and close her eyes, promising to sit beside her.

'Play it again, please—play it quietly—' Melissa pleaded, lying back on the pillows, and rather than cause further stress Sarah put the record on again, and sat by the bed with a book, praying her patient would fall into a merciful doze. After a while she did, and Sarah studied the lines of pain on the small face, and felt her heart ache for this unhappy girl, who only seemed to care for music and horses. But as yet Sarah had not liked to mention horses because of the accident.

When her patient woke, minus headache but full of dark and mysterious thoughts, Sarah offered the heavy-eyed girl a glass of fresh orange juice, delighted to see half of it gulped down thirstily. Melissa also consented to be wrapped up in blankets and taken into the garden in her wheel chair, and Sarah, her old sheepskin turned up round her face against the cold air, pretended not to notice the girl's silences and admired the gardens out loud ... the sweeping smooth lawns and secluded rose garden, the great trees and beautifully tended shrubs.

She decided that twenty minutes was enough, for the first time, and was pleased when Melissa actually wondered what was for tea, which turned out to be delicate ham sandwiches, hot-house tomatoes and home-made chocolate cake.

'I'll get fat,' Sarah announced as she licked the icing from her fingers, and Melissa shook her bright head.

'You won't. You're not the type. Karen will—she's slim now, but she's got a round face, and once she stops working all that muscle will turn into fat.'

Sarah absorbed this information in silence, but felt an absurd glow of pleasure. Poor Karen with the queer name—horrible, lissom Karen, who got taken out to dinner by

Jonathan. Dr. Lord, she corrected herself—and stop being so silly, Sarah! You know you don't even like him. Which was very strange, and a trifle confusing.

Melissa's good mood soon evaporated after tea, and Sarah's patience was sorely tried until Miss Gresham arrived to relieve her.

Was it her imagination, or did the older nurse's pale blue eyes hold a new look—an expression of mixed curiosity and dislike? Had her nephew been telling her about what happened—or perhaps Jonathan Lord had also become involved, expressing his disapproval of Staff Nurse Vane both to his partner and Evelyn Gresham. You're getting a complex, Sarah admonished herself, after she had given her report to Miss Gresham and told her that Mrs. Ruddy would relieve her later on for her meal break. She looked forward to a change of clothes and the evening free, and perhaps a walk in the fresh air.

The talk at dinner was safe and impersonal, until they were having coffee. In deference to her employer Sarah passed over the old jeans and shirt she would have liked to wear, and put on a brown cashmere sweater and pale beige velvet skirt. The meal was beautifully cooked, and Paul Courtney was an undemanding companion, telling her a little about his day at the cattle market, asking about his daughter, seeing to Sarah's needs at the table with impeccable courtesy.

They took their coffee over to the great log fireplace in the main room, as the night was becoming chilly, although the rooms were adequately heated, and Sarah lay back in the big leather chair, her hand on the red silky head of Bess, the old setter bitch.

She asked Paul if he would like Melissa to take some of her meals in the main part of the house—tea with her father, for instance, when he was in—supper by the fire, where she could chat to him.

'She needs to get out of that room sometimes, Mr. Courtney. I'm sure Dr. Lord will agree. She'll have to come in the wheel chair, which might make her like that more—and then perhaps she'll agree to go outside in it. She needs the fresh air—she's not eating well.'

Paul Courtney thought this was a good idea and told Sarah to do as she wished.

'I just want her to get better, Miss Vane.'

Sarah sighed. 'I know. I just wish that she—'

'Was not so unhappy?'

Surprised to hear it put so bluntly, Sarah nodded.

'Heaven knows I've tried,' he went on. 'She misses her mother, although it's such a long time—'

'Her mother? Is she—?'

'She's alive,' he said quietly. 'She left me,

left the child and me, in February, eleven years ago.'

Sarah waited in silence, knowing it was best to let her employer continue in his own way.

'She couldn't settle here, in the countryside. She was, and still is, like a butterfly, or a bright flower, Miss Vane. She has to have warmth and colour around her ... people, admiration—drama, I suppose.'

'Is she an actress?'

Paul Courtney shook his head. 'No. Oh, no. My wife is a singer. A very good one. She trained when quite young in Italy and Germany. I suppose she got used to travel and excitement in those days. Now she travels all over the world—'

Sarah caught her breath. Of course, how dense she had been!

'She's June Dennis! Melissa has her records ... we were playing them earlier today.'

Paul Courtney nodded. 'So you see, Miss Vane, my daughter has a mother who is famous and beautiful. I have tried to explain to her why—why June went, why I had to let her go—you can't cage a wild bird and watch it slowly die in captivity.' His voice faded away and for a while he gazed sombrely into the flames. 'She comes here to see Melissa—several times a year—she knows she can come whenever she wishes. The subject of divorce has been brought up, but—' He shrugged and smiled thinly. 'I apologise for burdening you with all this—'

Sarah shook her head. 'Please don't. After all, it will help me to understand Melissa. I think she needs to see people. It's a pity all her school friends are at boarding-school. Would it be possible—' she flushed, feeling that she was treading on delicate ground—'for her mother to come?' But she kept her chin high and met Paul Courtney's level gaze.

'It would be, Miss Vane. My wife is coming for Melissa's seventeenth birthday party next month.'

Sarah smiled. 'Oh, that's fine. I didn't know—'

'She seldom talks about her mother,' he said. 'But there is someone who will visit her—I've arranged it—he never fails to cheer Melissa up, although I'm blowed if I can see what they have in common—he doesn't ride, isn't musical ... blessed if I can understand it!'

'Anyone will do,' Sarah said cheerfully. 'As long as they—he, can cheer her up.'

Paul Courtney rose from his chair, standing with his back to the flames, hands deep in his pockets.

'Aye, you're right. It's young Philip, young Dr. Gresham. If I'm not mistaken you two have met, so between the two of you she'll soon be herself again. I've asked the lad to come whenever he can, as often as he fancies, so that's fixed. It'll be a grand bit of help for you, Miss Vane, to have him around to cheer her up.'

Wishing to post a letter home, Sarah asked her employer about the nearest post box, and he told her it was at the village shop, about a mile down the lane.

She felt the need to be alone for a while, and she slipped on her coat and made her way down the drive and through the great wrought-iron gates, on to the road, dark and silent under the overcast sky. Her thoughts chased each other round in her mind ... snatches of words, the faces of Melissa and her father, Philip Gresham, and the dark, watchful eyes of the senior partner, Jonathan Lord, who disapproved of her and what she was doing.

She found the post office amidst the dark huddle of village roofs and closely curtained windows and turned back, looking foward to an hour with a book before she slept. A big car slid darkly to a halt beside her and Jonathan Lord leaned out of the window.

'A trifle dark and late for a town girl, Staff Nurse. May I offer you a lift to the gates?'

Something in Sarah urged her to respond, to climb in beside him and let him take her in warmth and security back to the house, but she lifted her chin and gave him her best professional half-smile.

'I'm walking for my health, thank you,

Doctor. And might it not be safer alone out here than on a London street at night?'

A flash of white teeth in his dark face indicated that Jonathan was in an amiable mood.

'I've been on a case,' he observed mildly. 'A young mother in the village is due shortly. I've a feeling it may be sooner than later ... a bit early, in fact.'

Sarah felt her interest quicken, but made no comment on what he'd said.

'It's cold,' she remarked, and began to walk off. 'Good night, Dr. Lord.'

'Good night, Staff,' he replied, a faint note of amusement in the deep voice. 'I won't be in tomorrow, but my partner will make a social call on Melissa.'

Sarah halted and turned towards the car.

'Very well,' she said quietly. 'Philip and I know each other.'

He nodded. 'Yes. And although it is none of my business, Staff, except that he is my partner in this practice and you are working with me at Courtney Place, I would tell you that Philip Gresham is not—' he paused, searching for words—'carrying a torch for you any longer would perhaps be a handy way to put it, Staff.'

Sarah gasped in the friendly darkness.

'No, indeed,' he continued. 'The past is forgiven, and he forgave you for walking out on him ages ago. You acted impulsively perhaps—but we all do, when we're very young.'

Sarah stared at him in astonishment. 'Walking out . . .'? Philip no longer 'carrying a torch for her'? Was the man mad?

'But I—' she started, but he interrupted.

'I don't want to hear, Staff. You have work to do and so have I. Dr. Gresham is heart-whole and fancy free. And very popular, I might add, with the nurses up at the General! Have no regrets, my dear girl. Enjoy your walk and watch out for the long-legged beasties!' And he let in the clutch and pulled smoothly away, leaving Sarah open-mouthed in the lane, her eyes wide with anger.

As she walked swiftly towards Courtney Place she kept her head down against the wind, trying to think calmly. It was obvious that the general impression after her departure from the Northern General had been that she was turning down Philip Gresham, when in fact she had been fleeing from the humiliating fact that he had no desire for a serious relationship with her . . . that marriage was far from his thoughts, unlike the young, trusting Sarah, who had worshipped the ground he walked on.

Why had Philip told everyone he was the injured party? It was hard to believe his motive had been to put himself in a better light and gain sympathy from his friends and colleagues. Anyway, Sarah told herself as she walked up the smooth drive to the front door, he was not like that. He might have been rather selfish and unperceptive, but he was not dishonest or even devious. But why?

As she drifted into sleep, Sarah told herself that she had no wish to rake up the past. Her relationship with Philip Gresham finished a long time ago, and what was more, Jonathan Lord could believe exactly what he liked, because it was of no importance. He disliked her enough anyway ... That had been obvious from the word go.

* * *

Just another day, Sarah told herself as she made her way to the sick-room the next day, and then she would be free to go to see her grandmother and brother. It would be fun to drive the small blue car to the cottage and tell them all her news.

She took Evelyn Gresham's report of the uneventful night, pleased that her patient had slept quite well, and decided she would have another attempt to arrange a hair washing session. She was watching her patient move awkwardly about the room on her one crutch, when Philip Gresham entered.

'Very good. Very good indeed,' was his comment, in the familiar light, good-humoured voice, and Sarah felt herself flush hotly as she halted Melissa's progress and put the girl into her big chair.

'Good morning,' she heard herself say, and knew that Melissa was watching them both with interest.

'Sarah,' Philip said, his face alight with pleasure ... genuine pleasure, she could have sworn, and he took her hand in his, telling her that she looked marvellous, and how good it was to see her. He said he had brought along the tonic prescribed by 'the lord and master', which feeble joke made Melissa laugh a lot and had the opposite effect on Sarah.

She was relieved when Philip offered to push Melissa around the garden in her chair. It was plain that the girl really did enjoy the young doctor's company ... that although she responded well to Dr. Lord's personality it was the junior partner who could make her sparkle, and as she tidied the room Sarah marvelled at the change in her patient.

Later that day, to Sarah's relief, Melissa herself brought up the question of suitable shampoos, admiring the bright gloss and silkiness of Sarah's own hair now swept back and folded into a neat pleat from which only a few soft curls escaped to infuriate her as she bent over her reports.

In no time at all, Sarah had enlisted little Margaret's aid, as four hands were needed, four quick, gentle hands on the tangled chestnut mane. A soft rubbing with heated towels and half an hour with a brush and hand-dryer, and Melissa Courtney stared at her reflection and frowned with astonishment.

Her hair fell in shallow gleaming waves below her shoulders and framed her face in tiny curling tendrils, and Sarah thought immediately of the lovely head and shoulders of June Dennis portrayed on the record sleeve.

'It's lovely, miss,' Margaret said fervently, and Melissa smiled.

'Thank you, Sarah,' she said, touching her hair with her good hand. 'It never looks like this when I do it,' and Sarah looked suitably modest and said that it was easy hair to do, and no trouble at all, which was true. And then to her astonishment the girl asked when she would be back from her off-duty.

'Lunch-time, day after tomorrow,' Sarah told her. 'Then I'll be doing a spell of nights, to relieve the others. You're getting so you don't need any real nursing, you know. You're a spoiled kipper, Melissa.'

This was an old adage of Helen Vane, and made the two girls fall about with helpless giggles, which pleased Sarah mightily, feeling as she did that it was laughter the girl needed more than anything.

Mrs. Ruddy came in at that moment, to tell them that a young man on a motor-bike was there for Miss Vane and what was she to tell him?

Motor-bike? Sarah puzzled, until she realised that it must be her brother, who was inclined to impulsive deeds just as she was.

'Does he look like me, but younger?'

Mrs. Ruddy nodded. 'Aye, now that you mention it, he does that.'

Melissa demanded to see Michael, and while Sarah rushed up to her room to change, Mrs. Ruddy insisting that she left immediately, Michael stood in the doorway and exchanged shy smiles with Melissa until his eye fell on the array of records and the barriers between them vanished.

When Sarah came down, case in hand, clad in cord jeans, green polo sweater and her sheepskin, the two heads, shining chestnut and the other dark like her own, were bent over the music centre and she noticed how carefully Michael moved when near to the girl's slender, handicapped figure, his thin face alight with interest and compassion.

'He's eighteen, and studying agriculture,' she told them all; Melissa, little Margaret lurking in the bathroom pretending to be tidying up and Mrs. Ruddy, who was enjoying it all. 'Could you please tell Mr. Courtney I won't be taking the car after all, and that I'll be back at lunch-time the day after tomorrow?' Michael confirmed he would bring her back, which brought a sudden flare of colour to Melissa's face, quickly hidden by her hair as she looked down at the record in her lap.

'Have a nice time,' echoed in Sarah's ears as she left, and for the first time since she started her duties at Courtney Place she felt a professional satisfaction with her work there, as she held on to Michael's narrow waist and they hurtled down the drive and on to the road. Melissa would still have her awkward moods, her headaches, her spells of depression and rudeness, but progress was being made, a relationship established ... nursing was wonderful.

Sarah was delighted to find Helen Vane making a remarkably uneventful recovery from her attack. She looked well, though a trifle thinner, and now seemed resigned to handing over the greater part of her domestic burdens to Hannah Hardy, the widow who now lived at the cottage and looked after Helen and Michael.

What with helping with the meals, talking to Michael and sitting with her grandmother, the hours passed quickly. Helen Vane insisted that Sarah should get some fresh air and exercise, and she put on old clothes and went for walks down the old familiar footpaths.

The morning she was due to return to duty, Sarah sensed that her grandmother wanted to talk to her, and she created an opportunity, knowing that a tranquil state of mind was essential for the older woman's health.

They sat by the fireside, and Sarah watched the thin fingers knitting a bright blue pullover, presumably for Michael.

'You said that Philip Gresham is Dr. Lord's partner,' Helen Vane said quietly.

'Junior partner,' Sarah said. 'But he's doing a very good job there. He's a good GP, Grandmother.'

The older woman raised her brows and shot Sarah a faintly ironic look, which Sarah did not miss.

'He is, honestly. I've nothing against Philip at all—that's all over and done with.'

'If you say so, dear. I don't want you to be hurt again.'

Sarah frowned. 'I won't be, for the simple reason I—I don't feel anything for him now—he's just another doctor. I even like him, believe it or not.'

'Well, well—'

'But there is one thing, Gran—'

'Go on, child.'

'Well—I get the feeling, from various sources, that people think I jilted Philip, before I left the General. I think that's the impression he likes to give about what happened, and it puzzles me.'

'And you haven't spoken to him about it—asked him?'

'I haven't had a chance yet. Not that it

matters much now, it's all so long ago—except that—' Sarah broke off, knowing that she could not continue and say: 'I think Dr. Lord has heard all this, too, and thinks that I'm a flirt—thinks I treated Philip badly in the past.' No, that would require too much explanation, and reveal that what Dr. Lord thought about her mattered. It did, it was true, but Sarah didn't feel ready to reveal this.

'—I don't really want to go into all that again. Better to let it all rest,' she went on. 'It doesn't matter what people think, now.'

Then she steered the conversation back on to less personal lines, but now and then, until the time came to climb back on to Michael's pillion, she knew that her grandmother was thinking about their talk, and studying her. It was a pity she had said even as little as she did, Sarah thought, as they sped back towards Courtney. Her grandmother was far too perceptive. She must realise that Sarah was trying to deceive both of them, but especially herself.

CHAPTER THREE

The days and nights passed uneventfully after Sarah returned on duty at Courtney Place. Jonathan Lord called nearly every day to see

Melissa, and pronounced himself well satisfied with her progress, although Sarah continued to be worried by her young patient's melancholy moods and lack of interest in her surroundings.

Sarah's brother Michael rode out to Courtney Place one fine evening, ostensibly to see his sister, but the two young people got on so well together that Sarah was able to find a good excuse to leave them together to laugh and whisper and play records. Philip Gresham came quite often and took Melissa out in the wheel chair and once in his car, but this brought on a severe headache, and Jonathan Lord forbade any further car rides for a while.

Melissa's behaviour towards Sarah varied. Sometimes she revealed good-humour and sweetness that made Sarah feel better, but at other times she snapped and sneered and it took all Sarah's professional self-control to avoid direct confrontation. The worst enemy was boredom. The girl was still not fully recovered from concussion, and also handicapped considerably by her wrist and leg plasters. Karen Ludvika, who turned out to be not a nordic blonde goddess but a golden-skinned brunette with ice-green eyes, and every bit as devastating as Sarah had imagined, came every third day to supervise exercises.

She wore tight jeans and pure silk shirts

that clung lovingly to her magnificent breasts and hips and shoulders. It was apparent that neither of the two doctors minded in the least giving her lifts from and back to the hospital where she was employed. Neither did they mind taking her to the village pub for snack lunches, or even out to dinner on their free evenings. To give Philip Gresham his due, he asked Sarah several times to go out with him for a drive, or a drink, or dinner, but she always managed to find some excuse, although they soon began to get a bit overworked. His manner towards her was warm and friendly and she knew she would soon have to make it plain she did not want his company off duty. And also she would have to ask him about the lie he had told about her departure from the General.

One day Sarah was reluctantly admiring the picture Karen made as she concentrated on Melissa, this time in thin silk scarlet shirt and cream jeans, her hair piled on top of her shapely head in a dramatic top-knot, her black brows elegantly winged above icy eyes. Sarah glanced up to find Jonathan Lord's eyes on her, very faintly amused, and she knew that he was reading her mind and she hated herself for disliking the amiable Norwegian so much.

When they left and she was putting on Melissa's one slipper and tidying the room she heard Jonathan say that he would see that the horses were ready that evening and Karen replied something to the effect that she wanted to 'learn the jomp very vell'. In the sudden silence Sarah stared out of the window, seeing nothing, wishing she could ride once again, wishing she could ride just once with Jonathan Lord on the black stallion beside her. Fool, she told herself, blinking back hot tears of anger and self-pity. Utter fool. And then she got the idea...

'They're going riding,' she told Melissa. 'Heavens, I wish—' She broke off artistically, and the girl stared at her from her chair by the window.

'What, Sarah? That you could ride? Can't you?'

Sarah shrugged even more artistically and shook her head, begging forgiveness from above for her fibs.

Melissa frowned. 'How awful! I mean, poor you! I can't imagine—' She broke off, studying Sarah carefully.

'Have you been on a horse at all?'

Sarah sighed pathetically. 'Oh, I've been on one, but I was scared! And there was no one to teach me, even though I'd always wanted to learn. Oh, never mind—it's too late now.'

She watched as Melissa pondered.

'I could teach you.'

Sarah laughed. 'How could you?' She busied herself at her desk in the corner, hoping against hope. It would be something to hold Melissa's interest, amuse and stretch her, and get her outside into the fresh air. It would be acting a lie, but worth it, in the end.

'I could. You could have Goldie. She's a mare—' They both laughed, but Melissa went on: 'She's quite young but very docile. I'd teach you the lot.' She got up awkwardly and stood looking out of the window. 'Look—you could walk up and down there, on that wide path. I could tell you exactly what to do from here, by the open window, or out there—'

'—in your chair—' Sarah said slowly, her eyes wide with what she hoped looked like amazement and wonder. 'Oh, Melissa, could you really? Would your father mind?'

'Mind? Why should he? It'll be fun, Sarah. It'll be great—I just can't wait—' Melissa was almost jumping up and down with excitement, her cheeks flushed, and Sarah had to calm her down and make her promise not to get too frantic.

And so Melissa Courtney taught Sarah to ride, for the second time in Sarah's life. Sarah's plan worked perfectly ... Melissa would eat all her breakfast, her mind already on the day's ride, which usually took place for half an hour taken from Sarah's lunch-hour. Sarah felt the sacrifice was worth it, and later when Melissa's father saw what was happening, and the change in his daughter's whole being, he told Sarah to take the riding-lessons time out of her duty time, as he considered it 'very fine therapy, a marvellous idea', as long as Sarah didn't mind.

'I'm teaching Sarah to ride,' Melissa told Jonathan Lord one day as he finished examining her, and he straightened up, put Melissa's scaphoid back in her lap with an approving tap on the plaster and gave Sarah a searching look.

'That's right, Doctor,' she told him. 'Apparently I'm getting quite good.'

'I think she's a natural rider,' Melissa told them solemnly. 'She looks quite good, when she remembers to keep her back straight.'

Sarah bit her lip and frowned, trying to look embarrassed.

The doctor thrust his hands into his trouser pockets.

'Well, well. What a good idea! Our Staff Nurse a horsewoman. This I must see, I really must.'

Sarah shook her head, no longer needing to pretend confusion, but he was as good as his word. At the very next lesson, that afternoon, he appeared just as Melissa decided they'd done enough for one session, and Tom Sanders came to take Goldie to the stables.

Sarah, in her polo neck sweater and cord jeans, a borrowed pair of riding boots on her feet, looked down at the doctor as he stood holding King Cole's bridle. How long had he been watching, and what was he up to? His face was devoid of expression as he looked up at her, but something in the way he veiled his dark eyes with hooded lids and thick lashes warned Sarah.

'You take Miss Melissa back into the house,' he told Tom. 'I'll look after Staff Nurse and the mare.' And he did. He mounted King Cole in one strong, easy movement, and bent down to take Goldie's reins. 'Okay, we'll take a walk to the stables, Staff Nurse,' he told her. 'Be a good girl and show the nice doctor how much you've learnt...'

Sarah had no choice but to obey, but when they were out of sight of the house, it happened.

Jonathan hit Goldie smartly on the flank with his open hand and shouted at her. The mare, naturally, took this as an open invitation to make off at top speed, and Sarah found herself going at full gallop across the smooth turf, riding properly, the wind tearing at her hair, in control of her mount but still reeling mentally at the shock. After a few moments her natural good horsemanship asserted itself, and she began to enjoy herself, galloping along the edge of a small wood, hearing the thunder of hoofs behind her.

After a while she reined in and finally brought the little mare to a halt beside some great oak trees. She slid from the saddle and spoke to Goldie, patting her neck and rubbing her nose, apologising for the false game she had been playing and telling her she was a lovely little mare. When the doctor dismounted near by she refused to turn towards him, but he looped King Cole's reins over a low branch and walked towards her.

'I was right,' he said quietly. 'It was a hunch, at first. But just now, when you knew that Melissa was not watching you, I was sure. I watched your hands and your feet—Melissa was right, you are a natural rider, Staff Nurse, but you were taught a long time ago.'

Sarah's eyes flashed. 'All right, so you win this time, Doctor. What if Goldie had bolted, and I'd been thrown? Yes, I can ride, but I haven't for a few years. I could have been hurt.'

He shook his dark head. 'Wrong. For one thing, this little mare wouldn't bolt, would you, my love?' He caressed the mare's head with his long-fingered, muscular hand, and Sarah turned away, her heart pounding. 'Also, I knew you could ride well. It showed, and I couldn't resist forcing your hand. You enjoyed your gallop, didn't you, Sarah?'

His proximity, his voice and the use of her first name served to confuse Sarah even more. Anger, humiliation and desperate pleasure at his nearness jostled for supremacy, and she took a deep breath and smiled, fighting for control. To show this man how he unnerved her, how he made her feel young and vulnerable and very insecure in his presence would be dreadful. Right from the very beginning she had feared his effect on her, instinctively knowing that this was a man who could both master and delight her. Now her foremost instinct was to hide this knowledge from him, if she could.

'Sarah? Are you all right?'

The sudden concern was more than she could bear.

'All right? Of course I am! It was all a plan to get Melissa interested ... jolt her out of her awful moods. I know how she feels about horses. I got the idea the other day—I let her think I wanted to learn to ride and it all fell into place. And it's working, if you don't spoil everything. You won't, will you?'

She had no idea how she looked when she made her appeal, her oval face flushed by the exercise and emotion, her soft hair wildly dishevelled. Slender and defenceless in her motley of riding clothes, but always defying him.

'Spoil everything? Of course I won't.' He raised dark eyebrows in surprise. 'It was a good plan. A trifle fanciful, but it's working. I've not seen our patient so full of beans for a long time.' He grinned suddenly and held Sarah by the shoulders. She tried to move away but he was too strong. 'You're a clever girl, Miss Vane from St. Benedict's. A kind girl, too.' He studied her thoughtfully. 'What a pity I don't really go for nurse-doctor relationships. I could easily be tempted—' He lifted her chin with one finger and smiled at the flare of temper in her wide eyes. 'No? Ah, I see you're not as kind as all that. Not even to poor Philip, who still enjoys your company, or would if you would let him.'

He dropped his hands and Sarah moved back, breathing rapidly. 'I don't go for nurse-doctor things either, Dr. Lord. Not any more,' she said shakily. 'I was young and silly then.' And you're older but just as silly now, a small voice jeered at her silently in her mind. If he had taken you in his arms a moment ago you would have let him kiss you. You would have kissed him back, and told him that you love him. But he didn't, thank goodness!

'I've nothing against Philip,' she went on, as he went over to King Cole and brought the stallion nearer. 'I just don't want to rake up the past, that's all. And it didn't happen as you seem to think.'

He shrugged. 'It's not my business. I apologise if I've been—well, a step out of line. You're a very pretty girl, and I'm off-duty when I ride.'

He held out his hand, and Sarah put her foot into it and he put her up into the saddle. He thinks you're pretty, the small silent voice told her. Well, so is Karen Ludvika . . . much prettier—but she was filled with a sense of surprise and delight at the things he had said to her. Nothing would ever take them away from her ... nothing, no matter what happened.

They made their leisurely way back to the stables, the doctor leading, and as they approached the house they reined in the horses. 'I'll go in now,' Sarah said. 'Do you mind taking Goldie to Tom for me?'

He dismounted quickly and held both sets of reins as Sarah dismounted, feeling glad of his proferred hand. For a moment he held her, so close that she could smell the tweed of his coat, the faint scent of cigars and the other smells of the doctor, fresh cleanliness and soap and disinfectant.

'I know about your grandmother—why you had to leave St. Ben's,' he told her. 'The medical grapevine works swiftly. I've said a lot of things that I shouldn't. Is it any use to say I'm sorry?'

She nodded her head, unable to speak, and then she was making her way up to the great house, knowing without looking back that he was watching her.

Nothing has changed, she told herself as she went inside through one of the side doors and up to her room to bath. Nothing has changed, and yet everything is now different.

She lay on her bed, her head buried in her arms, and fought back tears of fatigue and misery. If she had not come to Courtney

Place but had found another nursing post, she would not have met Jonathan Lord and fallen in love again. No, not again, for this was not like anything she'd felt before. This ache, this terrible longing bore no resemblance to what she used to feel for Philip Gresham. This, then, was love, but it bore no resemblance to happiness.

★ ★ ★

Philip Gresham had been visiting Melissa, who was very much down in the dumps, and had managed to make her smile over mid-morning coffee when he turned to Sarah.

'You're off early this afternoon, aren't you? Like to come for a drive? I must say you look as if you could do with a break.'

Sarah looked up from her paperwork, feeling somewhat at a disadvantage. Her patient was looking at her with an encouraging expression, as if to say 'Oh, do go, Sarah,' and she found herself saying that she would like that. Melissa had been particularly difficult the last day or two, refusing to answer when spoken to, pushing her uneaten food round her plate, being awkward about her regular outings in the wheel chair. So Sarah knew it would do her good, aware that she was feeling the strain a bit, refusing to admit to herself that the reason for her pale face and shadowy eyes was not work strain at all—she could handle Melissa standing on her head with her eyes shut. No, the reason was within herself, in her brain, her body and soul, not allowing her to sleep properly, giving her no peace ... the face and voice of Jonathan Lord, who didn't really 'go in for nurse-doctor relationships' and also disliked her as a person.

Even two or three hours with Philip might serve to make her forget.

Philip parked his car well off the winding, climbing road and they got out and began to walk towards the fell top. The late afternoon sun was slanting across the peaks and it was very quiet, just the faint call of a curlew wheeling far above them breaking the cold silence. Sarah sat down on a section of crumbling drystone wall and sighed.

'It's so peaceful here—so beautiful.'

Philip Gresham nodded, hunting through his anorak pockets for his pipe before replying.

'You still belong here, I reckon.' He studied her, in her old coat. 'Did you hate London?'

Feeling that the conversation had swiftly taken a significant turn, she hesitated. 'No, I liked it very much. It was quite different, but I was very happy when I settled down. I loved St. Ben's, and the work ... everything.'

'But no emotional involvements, I understand.'

Their eyes met, and in Philip's blue eyes there was genuine, friendly interest, nothing else. Sarah shook her head.

'No, nothing, Philip.' She smiled suddenly. 'Lots of friends, no lovers.'

He nodded, satisfied with her answer.

'One thing puzzles me,' Sarah went on. 'It's about the time I left the General—running away like the stupid idiot I was—' She paused.

'Go on, Sarah.'

'Well—Jonathan, Dr. Lord, seems to think that I turned you down, jilted you, when it was the other way round, really. Why should he think that? Not, of course,' she added quickly, 'that it matters. It's just a bit odd.'

Philip chewed his pipe for a moment then blew out a cloud of fragrant blue smoke.

'It was my doing, I'm afraid. After you had gone to London the SNO got me into conversation—said something about what a shame for the General to lose such a promising young SRN, and so on—'

Sarah listened, her arms clasped around her knees, her eyes on the face that used to mean so much, and now meant so little.

'You know what hospital gossip is like, Sarah. Everyone was talking about you. The SNO said she had no time for young nurses who "set their caps" at young registrars and couldn't take a bit of heartbreak—she waffled on about young nurses wanting marriage too early in their careers—oh, yes, she fixed me with her steely eye and said she was bitterly disappointed in you, and so on.'

Sarah bit her lip. 'She was right, Philip.'

He shook his fair head. 'Not really, love. You never "set your cap" at me ... what an awful expression that is! We were young and silly. Anyway, I told the SNO that she was misjudging you, that it wasn't like that. I went on about it being mainly my fault that you'd gone, and then she asked me if in fact you had jilted me. I went all embarrassed and she began to give me a good telling off, mingled with sympathy—but not much. She said that you had made the right decision, and that young doctors should not expect good nurses to let themselves be sidetracked from their work, and you became her blue-eyed girl who got away from the naughty registrar—'

He paused for breath, and Sarah stared at him in astonishment. 'And you did that for me? You let everyone think that?'

Philip grinned. 'Why not? My shoulders are broader than yours, Sarah. It worked out okay. Everyone thought "poor old Philip" and also that you were well rid of me. My Chief also gave me scant sympathy plus a dressing-down—but it all blew over very quickly, and I was none the worse, and you were down in London.'

There was a long silence, while both of

them let their minds return to the Northern General.

'It doesn't alter the fact it was all my fault,' Sarah said sadly. 'But it was nice of you to let the SNO think that about me, even if our close friends knew otherwise.'

'Those that knew said nothing,' Philip answered. 'I bet I know where Jonathan got his information from—Evelyn and the SNO, who has retired now, were, and still are, old nursing cronies. Aunt Evelyn will have told Jonathan.'

'Idle gossip,' Sarah said severely. 'He's no right to go prying into my past!'

Philip smiled. 'You ought to know that all nurses and doctors are Nosey Parkers, even Jonathan.'

Sarah raised silky brows in surprise. 'I don't believe it.'

Philip nodded emphatically. 'He is! There's not much he doesn't know about you, love.'

Sarah scowled down at her feet in the short rough grass. Dr. Jonathan Lord might know a lot about her, but nothing that really mattered. But Philip was speaking.

'D'you want me to put him right? Does it worry you? Does it, Sarah?' He bent close, studying her face carefully. 'I'll tell him, if you like.'

Sarah got to her feet and pulled her coat collar high round her face. 'It doesn't matter,

Philip. I don't really care what he thinks about you and me! Let him think whatever he likes, it doesn't matter.'

'Hey, don't get so uptight,' Philip said, getting up and taking her arm as they returned to the car. 'If it doesn't matter, fine!' But he cast a searching look down at her flushed face. 'Anything wrong, love? Anything I can do?'

Sarah forced a smile as he opened the car door for her. 'Not really, thanks. Just keep your boss's name out of the conversation, if you want to please me.'

'Annoys you, does he?' he asked as he drove out on the road. 'He's a great guy, Sarah. But I'll tell you one thing, he doesn't suffer fools gladly—'

'I was a fool,' she said quietly, chin deep in her coat collar.

Philip put one hand briefly on hers on her lap before reaching for her safety belt and buckling it. 'I was, too. I know now what a fool I was.'

'That makes two of us, then, but we're friends now, aren't we, Philip?'

He smiled as they headed back towards Courtney Place. 'Sure we're friends. You'll come out with me again, won't you?'

Sarah hesitated, watching as the drystone walls sped by them, the great slope of the fell lifting against the grey sky. 'I don't know, Philip. I just have to go home and see my grandmother as often as I can—I just don't know.'

He nodded. 'Okay, I understand. I just wish you were happier. If only I could help—'

She made no reply, and the conversation became general and impersonal as by mutual consent they dropped the subject of the past, and talked about Melissa Courtney, the joint practice, and various local medical matters.

That evening Sarah drove herself home to the cottage and stayed quite late, busying herself doing some baking and hanging some curtains which had been washed and ironed ready for the windows. She told her brother that Melissa wanted him to come to her birthday party the next week and he went very red and pretended to be immersed in his books, strewn all over the dining-room table, but managed to give the impression that he would try to come.

One fine morning, with the frost glistening on the lawns and trees, Jonathan Lord made his professional visit on Melissa and enquired of Sarah when her next free time was.

'This evening,' she said. 'Why, Doctor?'

'Because I will take you to the next village and we will have some good sherry, fine cooking and interesting conversation, Staff Nurse,' was his reply. When she tried to protest that she really ought to drive over and see her family, he smiled and shook his dark head, saying that he had to be at Nortondale himself that afternoon. That he would look in on Mrs. Vane and check that everyone was well and happy, and that she, Sarah, looked as if she could do with a little light entertainment.

Sarah was aware that her eyes were wide and her mouth slighlty open, but her main concern was to brace her shaking knees against the arm of Melissa's chair to prevent herself from falling to the ground.

'Oh, do go,' Melissa said, to add to the general atmosphere of bewilderment. 'She's been ever so gruesome recently, Jonathan! Really snappy sometimes.'

He smiled at his patient, seeming unaware of Sarah's reaction. 'And you haven't?'

'Oh, I have, too, but it's weird, with Sarah—'

Dark brows raised, he turned his regard on to the subject of all this, who was busy pretending to fold some already folded towels.

'Gruesome, Staff Nurse?'

'No, Doctor, not really,' she replied in a dubious voice.

It was arranged that Jonathan would pick Sarah up at seven o'clock, and she and Melissa spent a pleasant couple of hours deciding what she would wear, and how she would do her hair, which served to pass the morning and put the patient in a lively mood, which Sarah thought was worth all the hideous anxiety the idea of an evening spent in the doctor's company aroused in her.

A table for two was booked for them at the Fox and Hounds in Lower Courtneydale. Over glasses of delicious sherry Sarah found herself talking about her work and her own life with perfect ease, and later the bewhiskered landlord came to say that their food was ready, if they were. Sarah was led to a secluded table by an open log fire and was glad that she was ravenous when home-made cream of lobster soup came, followed by local roast lamb with vegetables from the inn's own garden, and old-fashioned oven-baked local apples done in brown sugar and topped with thick cream.

She knew that she should have limited her wine intake to one glass, but Jonathan Lord insisted on two.

'You need to relax sometimes,' he said. 'You may not do a lot of expert nursing with Melissa, but it's a demanding case just the same.'

Sarah considered this, looking down into her coffee cup. 'I suppose so. But I like her very much.' She would have liked to say that she felt sorry for Melissa, but thought a trifle confusedly that this would lead to complications, with Dr. Lord asking why, and so on.

'I went out with Philip,' she said simply,

and he nodded and said that he knew, and the subject was dropped. Sarah leaned back against the crimson cushions and knew that if she was never happy again, at least she would have this to remember.

It seemed as if she had known Jonathan Lord all her life, and that the misunderstandings and stress of the past weeks melted away. He was wise and funny, interesting and intensely human, and just to sit opposite him and hear his voice and watch his dark face was all she asked.

The wine and good food and heat from the log fire tended to bring on an acute attack of drowsiness, however, and the doctor suddenly announced that he had no intention of keeping her out late—with a quick glance at his watch—so would she like more coffee, or should they go?

Sarah replied: 'Go, please,' smothering a yawn.

She found herself tucked into the passenger seat of his big grey car and thought how different it had been when Philip leaned across her to adjust the seat belt. Now she found it necessary to hold her breath and close her eyes, so intensely did she feel Jonathan's closeness, his arm across her, intent on his task.

When they pulled up outside Courtney Place the light was still on in Melissa's window and Sarah asked Jonathan to come in and say good night to the girl.

Jonathan switched off the engine and turned to her, a big, dark figure in the faint light.

'All right, just five minutes with her, as she's still awake. I see Philip's car is still here.'

Sarah put her hand on the door handle, saying: 'They enjoy each other's company. Thank you, Doctor, for a lovely meal, for the evening—' but he took hold of her wrist and put her hand back on her lap, holding it still in his warm hand. She fell silent, her throat aching with the things she wanted to tell him, allowing him to turn her face to him with gentle fingers, feeling his kiss, cool and undemanding and brief, but very sweet.

'No. Thank you, my sweet Sarah. And now to young Melissa—'

He was out of the car and round to let her out very quickly, his big hand round her arm, leading her up the steps and through the big hall to the sick-room.

Their patient was already in bed, Philip Gresham standing beside her, his top coat on, ready to leave.

Flushed, starry-eyed, Melissa put down her beaker of warm milky drink.

'You came, I knew you would! What did you have to eat? Isn't it a lovely place? Daddy takes me there sometimes for lunch, in the school holidays, you know, before all this—I won twenty-five pence off Philip, Jonathan. Will you play cards with me next time?'

Dr. Lord smiled at all this, replying with a mixture of nods and astonished grimaces which made even Sarah laugh.

'Did you come back early specially to see me, and don't you like the way Sarah's done her hair? I helped her decide what to wear, didn't I, Sarah? Doesn't she look great in grey?'

Sarah pretended to adjust the curtains to hide her confusion, conscious of the two men's amusement, and the whole-hearted way the senior partner endorsed all the flattering comments.

'There was the tail-end of a gypsy horse sale on the village green,' she remarked, turning back to the group round the bed. 'There were some ponies, Melissa. You would have liked them.'

No one spoke, and Sarah, unaware of the dangerous ground on which she travelled, went on: 'I've not seen your pony yet, have I? Is he kept here? It'd be nice if—'

Melissa stared up at her, blue eyes wide and her thin face a dreadful ashen colour. Sarah automatically noted the one good hand clenched and bloodless against the white sheet, and then from the girl's colourless lips issued a dreadful sound, half moan, half scream.

'No! No, no, no!'

Her screams became louder and wilder, and Sarah bent over her, not knowing what to do, but Jonathan Lord brushed her aside with a muttered order to fetch his bag from the car. Sarah ran, past Mrs. Ruddy who had come to the door and stood, appalled by the awful screams, saying: 'My lamb, what are you doin' to my lamb, all of you?'

What have I done? Sarah kept asking herself as she opened the car door and picked up the black leather bag and ran back to the house. Philip Gresham was standing by the front door, his face set and pale, and he took the bag from her, returning to her from the sick-room straight away.

'Listen,' he told her, and along the length of the corridor leading to the sick-room Sarah could hear her patient. No longer the terrible screams but the sound of wild, uncontrollable weeping, and the softer sound of the housekeeper's voice, and Dr. Lord's deeper tones.

'Shall I go to her?'

The junior partner shook his head. 'No! No, Sarah, she won't let anyone touch her but Mrs. Ruddy. Jonathan says we must let her cry for a while—'

Sarah stared up at him as she lowered herself shakily on to a stool by the dying fire.

'Why, Philip? What happened? What did I do, or say—it was me, wasn't it?'

He nodded. 'You don't know, do you? You

really don't know! Oh, heavens, Sarah, why didn't someone tell you?'

'Tell me what?' Suddenly Sarah realised where it was all leading. 'I asked about her pony—' She put her cold hand to her face, aware that she was shaking from head to foot.

Philip Gresham went down on one knee and put his arm round her shoulders.

'Yes, Star Boy—they had to put him down, on the spot. He broke both forelegs ... I thought you knew.'

She shook her head, and turned her face against his shoulder, grateful for the hard warmth of solid bone and muscle clad in rough tweed. Philip held her close but she could not control her trembling.

'Melissa blamed herself, right from the beginning. She said she put him badly to the jump, something about the number of paces ... she adored that pony—'

Sarah took a deep breath and muttered: 'Oh, don't Philip.' The distant sounds of weeping were gradually diminishing, but not completely yet.

'Don't blame yourself, love,' Philip said gently. 'I suppose everyone thought someone else had told you. There was a sort of conspiracy not to mention Star Boy's name—oh, heck, Sarah—'

She pushed him away and sat up. 'I'm all right, Philip—' and Jonathan Lord spoke from near by, his voice curiously uneven.

'So I see, Staff. Off you go, Gresham, I'll stay with the patient and give her a tiny something to make her sleep shortly. Mrs. Ruddy is coping very well.'

Philip stood up, and Sarah saw that he was red in the face, and knew that Jonathan had seen Philip's arm round her, his cheek against her hair, heard his gentle reassurance. She stood up, too, and watched as the junior partner said sketchy good nights and went outside to his car, and she turned and stood looking down at the cooling ashes in the hearth, hearing the sound of the car fade into the night.

'Drink this and go to bed,' Jonathan's cold voice said, and he pushed a tumbler into her unwilling hand and stood sipping his drink, watching her curiously.

'I don't want it,' Sarah said, sitting on the arm of a carved wooden chair, wishing that she was a thousand miles away. 'It was all that sherry and wine that made me go shooting my mouth off about ponies.' His eyes were cold and analytical and she felt about six inches high, but she pressed on. 'I'm sorry. I'm really sorry, doctor. I had no idea—'

'So I understand,' he said coolly. 'Do as I say and drink that.'

He watched as she lifted the tumbler to her stiff lips and sipped it with a grimace of distaste—brandy, with only a touch of soda, but his authority was not to be denied, and she drank it down and stood up.

'Shall I go and say good night?'

He shook his head. 'Certainly not. But go on duty in the morning as if nothing had happened. Do you understand?'

She nodded, wishing that the look of cold distaste would leave his face, demoralised by the coldness in his voice. His opinion of her as a nurse had not been all that high, on the whole. Now it would be at rock bottom, and there was nothing she could do about it ... nothing. Poor little girl, poor Melissa, hugging all that misery and guilt to her as well as the pain and discomfort of her injuries.

Sarah knew that she would burst into tears if she had to go on standing in front of this man much longer, but he made the first move. He turned away, saying: 'Good night, Miss Vane,' in a manner that left no doubt whatsoever of his anger, and headed for the sick-room where at last blessed silence reigned, while Sarah climbed wearily to her bedroom.

CHAPTER FOUR

When Sarah woke before dawn she felt tired yet restless, and for a long time she sat by the window waiting for the grey dawn.

She must leave. She would wait until Melissa was in her walking plaster, and able to use her hand a little, and then she would go. She would tell her employer straight away that she was looking for another post, and that it was up to him to decide if Melissa would need another full-time nurse or not. Dr. Lord would advise him, anyway. She shivered, pulling her robe around her, and longed for the comfort of a hot drink. It was still a long time until breakfast, but it seemed an age since the meal at the Fox and Hounds. She felt no hunger, but the ever-vigilant nurse inside her knew that food and drink would help to dispel the dull sensation of fatigue and depression.

She was half-way down the great winding staircase when she heard soft footsteps, and saw the small figure at the foot of the stairs.

'Mrs. Ruddy! Is everything all right?'

'Oh, aye, Staff Nurse. She's deep asleep now, poor lamb. I decided I'd make a bit of tea and toast, and then I thowt I heard your door open, like.'

Sarah paused on the bottom step.

'I woke early—a cuppa would be marvellous. Let's have one together ... you show me where everything is and I'll do it for you—you've been on duty.'

In spite of the older woman's protests, Sarah insisted, and found herself enjoying the task of filling the kettle and putting it on to boil, setting out two beakers with milk and sugar bowl, and making toast.

The housekeeper sat down and watched her, a faintly embarrassed look on her round face.

'Couldn't you sleep, then?' she enquired.

Sarah shook her head, and concentrated on buttering the toast. 'Not really. Not after what happened last night.'

'If you ask me,' Mrs. Ruddy said, 'it was high time someone mentioned that there pony. Someone had to, one day. It were bound to upset the poor lass, but the day had to come.'

Sarah considered this pronouncement.

'You may be right, but it could have been done a bit more gently. I jumped in with hob-nailed boots, asking where he was, not knowing that he was dead.'

The other woman nodded.

'Oh, aye, you're probably right about that, but it's done with now, love. You weren't to know. No need to lose sleep if it weren't your fault, is there?'

'I should've known, Mrs. Ruddy ... I should've made it my business to know. Asked, found out. Thought about it first and found out. I'm a fool—' Where and when had she heard that before? Yes, the day Philip drove her up on to the moors, and they talked about Jonathan. 'I was a fool,' she had said, and meant it.

Mrs. Ruddy reached over and refilled Sarah's cup. 'Is it that Dr. Lord? Has he been on at you, lass? I wouldn't put it past him.'

She shook her head. 'Not really, Mrs. Ruddy.'

'I should think not. Miss Melissa's had a good cry and got it out of her system, the poor mite, and is none the worse, in my opinion. Sleeping like a little bairn she is, in there.'

Sarah stood up and began to collect the tea things.

'I'll see to them,' Mrs. Ruddy said, but Sarah ignored her, stacking everything neatly on the draining-board and putting away the bread, butter and sugar.

By then it was fully morning, and she went upstairs into the quietness of the landing, took a leisurely bath, made her room reasonably tidy and opened the window wide on to the new day.

When she went downstairs and on duty there would be the problem of Melissa, and her attitude about the previous night's incident. Sarah wondered if her patient would show resentment or positive dislike, or just merely withdraw inside herself, in a way she did so well.

In fact, Melissa showed little signs of anything amiss, appearing relaxed and rested, and prepared to try to eat her breakfast ... some of it, if not all.

Sarah took Jonathan's advice and made no mention of her tactless remarks or the storm which had followed, and the day followed its normal, uneventful course. But as she performed her various duties Sarah knew that her decision was the right one—that the time to leave her patient was approaching.

Jonathan came, just after lunch, and pronounced everything satisfactory, but his distant manner towards Sarah was a silent reproach, although he was in no way discourteous. It was hard to take, after the evening at the Fox and Hounds, the joy of his company and his good night kiss. Not much of a kiss, really, compared with others she had received, but bringing with it a rare sense of delight.

But now, all that was gone, finished. Her decision to leave as soon as Melissa's walking plaster was put on hardened as the day passed. After the party, she decided. Melissa would still have small plasters on, fading bruises and occasional headaches, but soon she would be nearly fully mobile. It was not a pleasant thought, leaving the girl. She had become fond of her, in a curious way ... fond of Paul Courtney, and Mrs. Ruddy and Margaret, and the beautiful old house ... the horses ... everything. But she was no longer needed there. She was a nitwit, a fool, and not to be suffered, gladly or otherwise by anyone, especially Jonathan Lord.

'Darling Melissa,

I was so miserable not having you here for the concert at the Festival Hall ... hope you received the packet of press cuttings, etc., I sent you.

Everyone seems to think it was a big success but it would have been lovely to have you there. I sang most of your favourites, as I'm sure you'll know—did I include a programme?—and it was great seeing Jonathan Lord. He took me out to supper afterwards, with that physiotherapist friend of his—what a great big tall creature she is—and it was just like old times ... well, almost.

Jonathan told me all about you—that you have a young nurse up from St. Benedict's to look after you, and he seems very pleased with your progress...

I'm longing so much to see you on your birthday. I shall be driving up ... I'm living in luxury here, all paid for by the sponsors—will phone your father when to expect me. I shall bring your presents with me ... can't believe I haven't seen you since I came to St. Benedict's and you were all strung up on pulleys, and bandaged, and looking awful.

I know you may find it difficult to believe, but I do love you, my darling. Lots of love and kisses from your Mother.'

Melissa sighed heavily, and Sarah, looking up from her reports, regarded her patient sitting in the big armchair by the window, the pale sunlight striking sparks from her cloud of hair.

'Nice letter?'

Melissa gave one of her characteristic shrugs, but under Sarah's steady gaze changed it into a wriggle and rueful smile.

'Not bad. From my mother. She's staying in London.'

Sarah raised her brows. 'She is coming for your birthday, isn't she?'

'Of course. She says Jonathan took her out to supper after the Festival Hall concert—'

Sarah controlled her expression with a distinct effort, hoping that she looked suitably impressed. Why was Melissa looking so amused, almost maliciously pleased?

'Go on, Melissa. Get it off your chest, love—'

Melissa shot her a quick look, disappointed that her small but delicious morsel was anticipated.

'He took Karen out, too! I'd love to have seen Mother's face!' Melissa grinned hugely. 'Both their faces!'

Sarah waited patiently for the tale to unfold. After all, everyone knew that the delectable Miss Ludvika had accompanied the doctor to Town for the concert. Why should he not take both ladies out to supper if he so wished? Indeed, why not the entire female population of the capital, if it would feed his outsize ego?

As she thought this, Sarah immediately chided herself for her own somewhat uncharacteristic lack of charity and respect. Why should she care whom Jonathan Lord consorted with, or where?

'Karen will have been all dressed up—she can look marvellous when she wants—' Melissa went on. And when she doesn't want, Sarah thought, remembering that smooth tanned skin and the effortless grace of the trained athlete.

'I'm sure she can,' Sarah had the grace to murmur, but was totally unprepared for her patient's next revelation.

'You see, Mother has always fancied Jonathan, and—'

The blood pounded in Sarah's ears as the implication sank into her mind. She was unaware that she was staring at Melissa, her eyes huge with horror.

'Oh, Sarah, don't look at me like that! I didn't mean—oh heavens, Sarah ... it wasn't because of him that she left ... she told me years ago she always had a "thing" about Jonathan. Oh, dear, Sarah—'

Sarah rose to her feet. Her patient was too excited, too agitated for her own good. She soothed Melissa with non-commital remarks and poured a drink of orange juice, hoping that her own face betrayed nothing. After all, Jonathan Lord was a very attractive man. The most attractive you've ever met, remarked the small silent voice inside her head. And it was her lot to listen as Melissa babbled on.

'The two of them, Sarah, glaring at each other, wanting to get him on his own—oh, I know Mother doesn't give a hoot about Jonathan really, but you must admit he's very dishy, and Karen's potty about him. Oh, gosh, I wish I could have been there to see it all—' and she went off into a wild fit of giggles, which made Sarah hope that a racking headache would not ensue. But the headaches were fast retreating, these days, and it was good to see Melissa so amused, even though her own face felt like a frozen, polite mask.

'Can't you just visualise it, Sarah? Both of them absolutely loathing each other and being terribly polite, and Jonathan doing his strong, silent, black-browed act?'

I can visualise it, Sarah admitted to herself, threading a fine needle preparatory to mending a small tear in Melissa's apricot nightdress.

'I think jealousy's fascinating, don't you?' Melissa remarked.

'Jealousy?' The girl's mind leapt from one subject to another like an antelope, Sarah thought, but anything was better than talking about Dr. Lord and his charms.

'Yes, sure.' Melissa was off again. 'Like Karen, and my mother.'

Sarah nodded, aghast but held captive by her own involvement.

'And Jonathan—I guess he's jealous, too.'

'Jonathan—Dr. Lord, jealous? Why should he be, for heaven's sake?'

Melissa nodded complacently. 'Oh, he's the type, those dark, sarcastic people always are.'

'Always?' Sarah asked faintly.

'Yes. Mind you, Sarah, he's pretty good at keeping La Ludvika at arm's length, haven't you noticed?'

'Can't say I've taken much interest,' Sarah lied, snipping the thread carefully and folding the nightdress. And does he keep the lovely June Dennis at arm's length just as successfully? she wondered. Did he play one woman off against the other and watch the results with quiet amusement? No, she told herself quickly. He was a hard man in many ways, a trifle inflexible, and not averse to a little quiet tormenting, but he was not cruel. Of that she was sure.

Sarah was off duty after tea, and she retired upstairs and took a long hot bath, but found herself unable to escape from the long and somewhat pointless dialogue with Melissa about the doctor, and her mother, and jealousy.

She wrapped herself in a warm long towelling robe and opened one of her text books, but try as she could she was unable to concentrate on the words.

Quickly she pulled on sweater, jeans and walking boots and her thick old coat and ran down the curving stairs. Soon it would be dark, but she had to be outside, beyond the confines of the gentle old house that was beginning to feel like a prison, just as her own unhappy thoughts were imprisoned inside her head.

Head lowered against the driving wind, Sarah walked beyond the village to where a small huddle of old cottages stood back away from the main road. Few people were about ... in the distance a dog barked and rooks cawed high in the swaying trees.

The car was parked almost exactly in the same place as it had been that other night when she came searching for the post box for her first letter home from Courtney Place. She remembered how she had wanted to give in to her instincts and accept Jonathan Lord's offer of a lift ... how she had been pert and even a little provocative, over-reacting to his irony when he called her a 'town girl'.

All this passed through Sarah's mind in a flash as she slowed down near Jonathan's car. He was sitting at the wheel, the window wide open, his thick dark hair blowing across his face and he watched her with no change of expression.

'Walking, Staff Nurse?'

Sarah nodded, forcing a smile, her heartbeats thudding against her ribs.

'Just walking, Doctor. Are you having trouble?'

He smiled. 'Not car trouble. Pondering over a case. Her name's Elizabeth Nixon ... she lives in one of those cottages.'

Sarah nodded. 'You were there that other night. You said then you had a feeling about her.'

Jonathan got out of his car and held the door open. 'How much ante-natal experience have you had, Sarah? Get in ... I'd like to talk about her to you.'

Sarah muttered something and clambered into the passenger seat and he got back in and rolled up the window.

'I'd get her to the hospital several weeks before the date but she's already got a two-year-old and a retarded older one,' he muttered, talking more to himself than to Sarah. 'So that's out. Her husband works on the farm every hour he can. He's good to her ... does his best.'

'What makes you so worried?' Sarah dared to ask, and he told her it was more a premonition than anything else. For quite a long time Sarah sat quietly by his side and listened, saying very little, knowing that what Jonathan Lord needed was a sounding board for his own impressions and theories, not the benefit of her somewhat limited obstetric experience. One day, she told herself, I'll study midwifery and perhaps get a rural job, health visiting or running a clinic. She found the look on Jonathan Lord's face very revealing. A look of deep compassion and caring, all of his highly trained mind turned inwards on to this one village family and their coming child.

'So you see, Sarah,' he said, 'Philip and I will keep a close watch. She can send a neighbour to phone for the ambulance or for me—'

'Or even me—' Sarah longed to say, but knew that it would sound absurd and unprofessional. But she knew she would like to assist him to deliver a child against an emergency setting, forgetting, for a few minutes, that he disapproved of her professionally ... and then she suddenly remembered the look of cold distaste on his face as they both listened to Melissa Courtney's wild weeping—the coldness of his voice, and the cold, correct courtesy of the following days.

Now, in the intimate warmth of his car, comfortable against the dark leather, Sarah knew that she would give anything to turn the clock back—to start again at the beginning when she first arrived. But even then was too late, for it had all started long ago, with

Philip, before she met Jonathan Lord.

'Fine, Doctor,' she heard herself say. 'I'll be getting back.' But he gently removed her hand from the door and drove back through the village, through the great iron gates and up the curving drive to the front door.

'Safe and sound,' he said. 'How do you feel about our patient now, Sarah?'

She wished that he would stop using her name. Better the formality of Miss Vane or Staff Nurse than the treacherous lurch of her heart as his voice dwelt on the two syllables.

'I'm pleased with her, Doctor,' she said, and then, plunging into deep waters, her hands tightly gripped together on her lap: 'In fact I'm planning to leave, as soon as she has her walking plaster. Get the birthday celebrations behind us, get her mobile. She won't need me any more; there's not enough real nursing to do anyway, is there? I can easily find another post—'

'In these parts, I presume?'

Jonathan's voice was low and controlled, and Sarah felt a sudden chill. If only she knew what he was thinking. Did he long for her departure? Was that it?

'Yes, I expect so. Certainly in Yorkshire.'

He nodded. 'Of course,' and for a moment their eyes met and their wills clashed. Not 'Oh, what a pity, Staff Nurse. I would like you to stay longer,' or, she thought wildly, 'Don't go, Sarah, I need you ...' Nothing except 'Of course.' Which was exactly what she should have expected.

Once he had kissed her, just once, and only briefly. And on another occasion he had lifted her chin with his finger and told her he could easily be tempted, as their horses cropped the short winter grass under the great trees. Now, all he could say was 'Of course,' and why not, when his life was full of available girls and women like Karen Ludvika and many others at the hospital...

'Have you told Melissa's father?' he asked, and she shook her head, wanting to tell him that she had told no one, that she had barely been able to find the courage to tell him.

'I will, soon,' she said. 'I'll give plenty of notice ... everything according to the book,' and she opened the door, hurrying so that he would not have time to get out and come round to help her.

'I see. Thank you for listening, and good night.'

'Good night, Doctor, thanks for the lift.' She walked quickly round the front of the car, but he climbed out and stood, tall and motionless, as she went up the steps. She longed to turn round and take a final look, to say: 'Good night, Jonathan,' but she clenched her hands in her pockets and leaned against the inside of the great doors after they had closed behind her and heard him drive away. She had never said his name to him, but now, as she climbed the stairs to wash and change for the evening meal, she said it over and over again as she put her foot on each shallow curving rise. Jonathan ... Jonathan ... Jonathan ...

CHAPTER FIVE

What to wear for the party occupied Melissa's mind quite well, on and off, for a whole day. Eventually Sarah persuaded her to wear an ankle-length printed dress in bright pleasant shades of blue and purple and gold, the full drawstring neckline and sleeves setting off her fine milky skin and bright hair and eyes.

She was now able to use both crutches, her fractured wrist bone healing with the miraculous speed of youth. She wrote endless lists of the food she wanted for her guests, young and old, and had long serious discussions with her father, Mrs. Ruddy and Sarah about which pieces of furniture or carpets to be removed, who was to sleep in which bedroom, and the music.

June Dennis arrived the day before the party. She seemed to fill every room with her presence ... here a silk scarf or soft handbag left in an armchair, there a book or magazine, and everywhere the subtle fragrance of expensive perfume.

Paul Courtney seemed to be content to let her pervade what used to be her home, watching her move in the house and grounds, listening as she and Melissa chatted endlessly about songs and musicians, concerts, travel, clothes, and more songs.

June treated Sarah with exactly the right mixture of friendly interest and the reserve between professional employee and employer's estranged wife. Sarah decided this was the end product of innate good manners, a good in-built sense of occasion developed through her life in the public eye, and a touch of Melissa's own sweetness.

It was a pity, Sarah thought, going off duty early next morning, at Evelyn Gresham's insistence, to prepare herself, wash her hair, do something about her short, scrubbed nails, that Paul Courtney had to be a farmer. Perhaps if he had been a country lawyer or business man June might have stayed . . . ever restless for her world of music but able to endure the compromise. But not here, at Courtney. Not here where the trees and the great fields stretched in every direction, and every activity was geared to the estate, the farms, the land. Paul was wedded to the land by his inheritance, and the tragedy of his love for Melissa's mother and June's own nature, and her bright shining flame of talent.

Sarah washed her hair and settled down to render first aid to her hands—plenty of soothing cream and a fair imitation of a professional manicure, finishing with two coats of pale pearly polish which made her newly oval nails look quite pretty, if not glamorous.

She had offered to lend a hand in the kitchen, where a great deal of baking and preparation was taking place, but had been shooed upstairs by Mrs. Ruddy, who had got in several old friends from the village to help out.

On her bed in her towelling robe, drying her hair with a hand dryer, Sarah tried to calm her steadily rising panic. If there was any way she could have escaped the coming party she would welcome it, but apart from dire ill-health there was no way out. As she began to dress there was a knock on the door and Mrs. Ruddy stood there with a small tray of tea and toast, pointing out that Sarah had not been down for tea.

Sarah exclaimed: 'Oh, Mrs. Ruddy, you are a dear! There are so many people in the house—I felt—I just felt I'd rather—'

The housekeeper tutted and put the tray down and cast a look round the room.

'Is it warm enough in here, love? There's a fair cold storm blowing up out there and, heavens above, the rain! Never stopped for nearly three days, it hasn't!'

Sarah poured her tea and agreed it was a miracle that the guests from far afield had managed to get there. She knew Michael would manage it on his bike through hell and high water, but she would make sure he didn't stay too late, with that long ride back to Nortondale.

Fortified by the hot tea and Mrs. Ruddy's comforting chat, she showered quickly and laid out her clothes on the bed. The dress she had bought for the last staff ball at St. Ben's was all she had that would do, and she stood in her brief lacy panties and held it up in her hands. Melissa has seen it, and her comment had been 'smashing', said with a certain degree of surprise. Perhaps she had not visualised Staff Nurse Sarah in soft, drifty grey chiffon, with narrow silvery shoulder-straps, after her severe uniform dresses, sweater and jeans.

Her hair had dried in soft shining waves, falling loosely nearly to her shoulders, with one wayward lock across her brow which refused to be disciplined. She applied make-up carefully, bronze eyeshadow, lip gloss in soft carnation pink, and just a touch of perfume... Sarah, Staff Nurse Vane, up from London, all done up and nowhere to go, and determined to pretend she was longing for this party...

Downstairs everything was in full swing. There were flowers everywhere and great log fires in every room. Coming slowly down the staircase Sarah heard the deep hum of many voices, laughter, music, saw her brother's big grin and was enveloped in a quick hug.

'You look super, Sarah. So does Melissa ... isn't her mother great?' And he was off, looking very handsome, she thought proudly, with his fair hair and slim, sturdy physique, and his big smile.

Paul Courtney appeared by her side with a drink for her and introduced her to a lot of people, after Sarah had insisted on finding Melissa and wishing her a happy birthday formally. She had done this earlier in the day, and given her patient a sweater in soft blue cashmere, but it seemed right to seek her out where she sat surrounded by relatives and friends, and kiss her flushed face and say it all again.

People were dancing and very soon Sarah found herself on the floor, dancing with strangers and people she knew .. once with Philip Gresham, who said he had just popped in to say hello to Melissa and had to get back on duty.

Sarah finished her first drink and found that she was enjoying herself. The music was good, the room looked beautiful, Philip had whistled softly when he first saw her, and she loved to dance.

Jonathan Lord was easily head and shoulders taller than Melissa's mother and a good six inches taller than Sarah, but when he took Karen Ludvika's hand and pulled her towards him and spun her round, his dark face was not far from her lovely laughing one. He was a good dancer, Sarah noted dully, moving with economy but flawless rhythm.

She wandered away from her last partner and found a low stool and a little table where she could put her drink. She was called back to dance, but she shook her head and fanned her face with one hand, and reached for her drink. How could she dance when he was there, when she might brush against him, when he would see her in her absurd dress and sandals, her face painted and her hair loose and wild.

Idiot, she told herself. She was no more elaborately dressed than anyone else, so why should she care how he saw her? What difference could it possibly make?

Now he was partnering June Dennis and very beautiful they looked together, the big dark man and the tiny flame-haired woman, barely beyond her middle thirties, delicate and vital in black silk blazer and long slit skirt, everything about her shouting of capital cities, glamour and fame.

A little later June sang for them. Melissa beckoned Sarah to sit beside her, and slipped her small hand into Sarah's as they listened to the lovely voice. Everyone laughed and clapped and called for more, and yet more, and eventually June Dennis shook her bright head, and said 'enough'.

As she was singing, Sarah turned her head to catch her brother's reactions, and inadvertently found her eyes gazing into those of Jonathan Lord, who was standing by himself in the doorway. He studied her for a moment, taking in Melissa's hand in her own, and it seemed to Sarah that he nodded very slightly.

He crossed the floor and she felt his strong fingers round her waist.

'Dance, Sarah?'

The music was Latin-American, fast and intricate, and Jonathan found a corner which he commandeered so that they had room to dance. She moved softly to the beat, knowing that people were watching them, some even clapping to the rhythm, feeling her soft skirts swirling against her legs, her hair floating, her senses reeling when he touched her. Then silence, and scattered clapping.

'Very good,' Jonathan Lord said, looking down at Sarah.

'Yes.' There was nothing else to say. He was right, it had been very good.

Karen linked her long brown arm through the doctor's.

'Jonathan, I haff to spik vith you.'

Sarah was aware that the evening was passing very swiftly. Michael came and told her that he was leaving ... She glanced at her watch and was surprised to see it was nearly eleven.

Melissa was saying good night and thank you to everyone, and Evelyn Gresham hovered in the doorway in uniform, waiting to put her charge to bed. June linked her arm through her daughter's as they made their slow, awkward way across the room.

'Good night,' Sarah said. 'It was a lovely party.'

Melissa nodded, too tired to reply.

'I'll see her to bed, Sarah, and then my—her father is going to drive me back to London. I won't be long, Paul,' June Dennis said.

Everyone was leaving, except for a few hard-core older teenagers who looked set for another hour or so of records and dancing.

June Dennis came back, a warm waterproof coat over her finery, her suitcases ready side by side. Paul Courtney, in his raincoat and old tweed hat, said good night to his guests and to Sarah, saying he would be back the following evening.

'You'll be tired tomorrow,' he told Sarah. 'And so will Melissa. Take it easy. The weather's terrible, so keep yourselves cosy. I've left my phone number with Mrs. Ruddy.'

Sarah smiled, taking all this in, wishing she could politely escape. Melissa's mother stood on tiptoe and kissed Jonathan Lord and gave him one of her warm smiles. Karen, standing close to the doctor with a white coat thrown round her shoulders, scowled and drew nearer to him. He will drive her back to the hospital, Sarah told herself. Or perhaps to his house for a nightcap, or perhaps they will sit in his car and he will kiss her.

Glad it was over, Sarah faded into the background as the crowd filtered out of the great front doors and down the steps into the wild wet night. Already most of the supper debris had been cleared away and the fires banked down and main lights turned out, and Sarah went slowly along to the side wing where Melissa's room was.

Her patient was already in bed, the lamp turned low, and Sarah contented herself with a quick kiss.

'It was super,' Melissa said sleepily. 'I hope Michael will get back okay.'

'Oh, he will. It's a main road all the way,' Sarah reassured her.

'There's a lot of water about,' Sister Gresham remarked from her report table. 'When Jonathan brought me tonight from the cottage the river was coming up fast. He said he'd go back the long way, by the main road—' she gestured towards the garden and the woods beyond. 'The lane short cut will be under water by now.'

Already Melissa's eyes were closed, and with a smile at the older woman Sarah crept out. The house seemed very quiet, and she saw that the light under Mrs. Ruddy's door was out, on the top landing. Two asleep and one to go, she thought, pausing to look through one of the uncurtained windows on the long gallery, unable to see anything in the darkness through the vicious spatter of wind-driven rain.

She shivered slightly, looking forward to a warm bed, a short read, and, she hoped, sleep.

Sarah had no idea how long she had been asleep when Evelyn Gresham came into her room. She was awake instantly, aware of the other woman's urgency, every sense alert.

'Get up,' Sister Gresham was saying. 'We've an emergency on our hands. I can't cope alone now that Melissa's woken up.'

Sarah jumped up and pushed her feet into mules.

'Emergency? Melissa's all right?'

'Of course she is, but I need you. Hurry up and come downstairs.'

They hurried down, to where a man stood in the hall. A young man, tall and thin, with water streaming from his wild hair and strained white face, dripping from his clothes and boots on to the polished floor.

'I had to come to the front door,' he said apologetically in a strong local accent. 'Couldn't make anyone hear back there—' he inclined his wet head towards the kitchen regions. 'It's the wife, Nurse, miss—' He looked from one to the other, not knowing whom to address.

'The cottages by the green?' Sarah asked. 'Her third baby—Dr. Lord?'

Evelyn Gresham said that she knew about that one, that the doctor had been having doubts. Sarah stared at the man. He must be an idiot ... he should be telephoning the hospital so that they could come and get his wife ... he already had two children, he must know the drill.

'The lines are all down or summat,' he said quickly, as if reading her thoughts. 'I tried the phone box on the green and then knocked me neighbour up. He's an old chap, lives on his own ... his is dead an' all.'

A few questions from Sister Gresham, who had qualified in midwifery more years ago than she cared to remember, ascertained the mother's condition. Frequent contractions, coming and going. Considerable bleeding ... vomiting ...

'She's scared, Nurse. She weren't scared when she had t'others. It's a month early, I reckon ... '

Mrs. Ruddy appeared in the doorway, wrapped in a red dressing-gown, her white hair in rollers.

'Our telephone's out of order, too,' she announced. 'No use trying to ring t'hospital from here.'

'It's all them trees blown down,' the young man explained. His thin face was white and strained, water dripping from his cap. He was wet through, his trouser legs torn and dripping water, his boots oozing water and mud. 'We got to do summat,' he muttered. 'What we goin' to do?'

'One of us will come back with you,' Sarah said. 'But we've got to get to a phone. Haven't any of your neighbours got a car?'

'Oh, aye, t'old feller next door. But like I said, there's trees down. One's right across the lane, blocking his gate. There's a couple down on t'main road as well ... I were forced to climb over them, like, to get here. The lanes are regular rivers...'

'I'll go to her,' Evelyn Gresham announced. 'It's no use trying to stop me, child. If the young man can get here then he can take me home with him.'

Sarah nodded. It was true, one of them had to get to the patient, and even if Sister Gresham was over sixty she was a tough old bird ... and a midwife.

'What's your name?' she asked the man.

'Charlie, miss. Charlie Nixon. The wife's called Elizabeth.'

They watched as Evelyn got into her mac and boots and tied a scarf round her grey hair.

'There's water all over,' he said anxiously. 'And bits of trees.' But Evelyn was undeterred.

'Never mind that.' She turned to Sarah.

'Can't that man Tom Sanders get over to the cottage to Jonathan?'

'He's not here,' Mrs. Ruddy interjected. 'Gone off to a horse sale or summat. There's no way to get to Dr. Jonathan anyway, as I see it. This lad 'ere says the main road's all water and fallen trees, and I reckon the short cut through the park and over the woodland'll be under water ... the stream's been in flood since yesterday.'

Sarah nodded. This just confirmed her worst fears. But they had to get to a telephone somehow, to get full medical help out to Elizabeth Nixon and her premature baby. One handicapped child in a family was enough, and this child was already in desperate danger.

'You go, then,' she told the older nurse. 'I'll think of something. Good luck, both of you.'

Charlie put on his dripping cap.

'I'll look after 'er,' he said. 'Wish we could find a phone, like ...'

'King Cole, Sarah.' Melissa stood in the unlit part of the hall, supported on both crutches. 'He'd take you to Jonathan, like a shot.'

Sarah felt her mouth drop open in astonishment, but she pushed Charlie Nixon and Sister Gresham towards the front door.

'Go on, you two. This might be the answer, although ...'

For a moment she watched as the two figures disappeared into the rain and darkness, the wind tearing at them, buffeting them from side to side. Then the darkness surrounded them, and Sarah found herself praying that they got back soon to the woman in labour.

'Don't you worry—' the houskeeper said from behind Sarah, waiting to shut the door. 'They'll be all right. Evelyn's a good 'un. She was on the district as a young woman, and then in the army ... she's seen worse'n this, Sarah.'

Sarah nodded. 'I know. But she's got nothing with her ... no midwifery kit—'

'She'll be there, that's the main thing. That poor lass'll know she's got a nurse with her—'

Melissa interrupted impatiently: 'Are you or aren't you going to, Sarah? King Cole knows the way ... he's taken Jonathan down there, and my father, loads of times. He's not afraid of water, or the dark...'

'What makes you think I can phone from there?'

'It's a chance. I've heard Jonathan say that they're on a different line, or something. Once when theirs wasn't working Philip came up to phone...'

Sarah bit her lip. 'I can't ride that horse.'

The girl gave her an icy-blue stare.

'You're going to try, though, aren't you? You've no choice. It's not far, and you've got to get through to the ambulance, or at least get a doctor to Mrs. Nixon.'

To Sarah it seemed that there was a tone almost of contempt in Melissa's voice, and this made her angry.

'How do I get on to his back? How do I tell him where to go?'

'Go and put some warm clothes on,' Melissa Courtney said patiently. 'Heavy shoes, not boots. Boots might fill with water and then you'd be in trouble. And stop panicking.'

'Not boots,' Sarah said obediently, starting to go upstairs, holding her robe up in one hand.

She scrambled quickly into a thick old sweater and her oldest slacks, with heavy walking shoes over warm socks. She pushed her hair up roughly into a red knitted cap pulled down well over her ears and found her riding gloves and a torch, and wondered what Jonathan Lord was doing at that moment.

Melissa was waiting in her wheel chair, clad from head to toe in her father's heavy-duty oilskins. She held out a heavy khaki jacket, which Sarah put on and zipped up, turning the hood up over her woolly cap.

Mrs. Ruddy, clad in her old mac, helped Sarah to lower the wheel chair down the front steps and they headed for the stables.

Sarah asked: 'Are you sure King Cole knows the way?'

'I'm sure,' Melissa replied.

'How do I get on to him?'

'You'll see.'

The black stallion watched as Sarah and Mrs. Ruddy piled bales of straw on top of each other. At first he laid back his ears and showed the whites of his eyes, but Melissa got out of the wheel chair, supporting herself against a wooden partition, and held his head and kissed him, whispering in his ears.

Together they managed to put on a bridle, but to saddle him was a different matter.

'I don't think he'll let us,' Melissa said. 'Even if we could, which I doubt. It's a very heavy saddle. The one you use for Goldie won't do.'

Sarah eyed the stallion, who returned her gaze intelligently but without malice.

Melissa pointed to a rack of folded blankets.

'Put that blue one on his back. Yes, that's right, it fastens on. Climb up on the bales, Sarah, you're about to be launched.'

Speechless, Sarah perched on the top bale and looked down at the immense back in front of her. Bare-back into the dark night rode the young nurse ... now she had seen it all.

She glanced at her watch, and was astonished that barely half an hour had elapsed since Charlie Nixon poured out his tale to them ... it seemed like hours.

'Down the path through the park,' Melissa was saying. 'You've been there before, with Jonathan.'

So I have, Sarah thought, but how do you know?

'Just point his nose in the direction of the cottage, tell him to take you to Jonathan and keep him on the go. He knows the way, or he'll jolly well find another one.'

'He'll be afraid of the wind and the rain, and the water,' Sarah went on, lightly sliding on to the blue blanket, feeling the incredible strength of the horse beneath her.

'No, he won't. He's not afraid of anything, this one. You have to trust him, Sarah. He'll trust you and you have to trust him.'

'What if I fall off?'

Melissa gave her a sneer. 'The way you ride? Never. Don't be an idiot.'

It was then that Sarah knew. Melissa had not been fooled for long.

'When did you know?'

'About after two lessons. I went along with it, though. It was fun, wasn't it?'

Sarah stared down into the small white face, the uncombed wet hair, the blue eyes.

'Yes, it was fun. I—I thought it'd be good therapy for you—'

The girl grinned. 'I know, it's okay, Sarah. It's time you were off. I've already told him to go to the cottage. All you have to do is sit there nicely, keep his nose pointed in the right direction and trust him. Right?'

Sarah said right, and waved them good-bye as she walked the stallion out into the night, along past the shadow of the house and then turned her back to the lighted windows and comforting walls and roofs, away towards the path through the park, the narrow lane between the fields and the short cut through the woods. And the stream, which was now a river...

No light appeared in the distance. King Cole seemed quite pleased to be let out on such a strange night, so black and wet, the trees tossing themselves all around them in a fury. She could tell by the stallion's gait that the ground underfoot was wet ... very wet, and several times he halted and stood as if deciding which way to go, before obeying her gentle words.

Sometimes she had to bend almost double to avoid being knocked to the ground by low boughs, and she knew that King Cole had left the normal path and was in some mysterious fashion finding his own way. Ahead she could hear the sound of rushing water, a loud, ominous sound that chilled her. But if she could hear it so could her mount, she decided, and she gave him his head and let him walk on.

And then, suddenly, she felt King Cole slither sideways, scrambling for a foothold with his hoofs, and she knew by the unmistakable sensation of icy water up to her ankles that they were in the stream. The stream which was now a river, dark, fast-running, treacherous.

Fighting with the panic inside her, she spoke to the stallion, trying to find comfort in the fact that he heard her voice. She leaned forward and patted his huge, dripping neck, feeling cold trickles of water running down her own neck and inside her clothing, but nothing mattered now, except to get to Jonathan.

After what seemed an eternity of freezing water, the deafening sound of wind in the trees and howling against her ears, and very little progress, King Cole reached the far bank of the torrential stream, now swollen to a fast-flowing river.

He clambered up the slippery bank as if he knew exactly what to do without Sarah's guidance, and she felt by his progress that they were once more on dry land ... if you could call anything there dry, she thought grimly. He picked his way sure-footed through the wild, tossing darkness, making his own path, and she bent down and kept her face close to his mane, to protect it from overhanging branches, and prayed that nothing would happen to sweep her from his broad, warm back. For once dismounted she would never be able to climb on to him again without help.

She urged on King Cole, and then saw a light, shining through the trees. Thank heavens, a light...

'Look, King Cole, a light—we're nearly there...'

She was not aware that now tears mingled with the rain on her face, and the mud, and the blood from a cut on her forehead where a branch had scraped her.

She remembered very little, looking back on the incident in days to come—how she urged the horse on, and they finally emerged on to the country lane, King Cole taking the wide, flooded ditch with his easy stride as he made for the cottage.

She remembered praying that someone would be there in the cottage, and that it was not just a hall light left on in a deserted place, to deter intruders.

She slid from the horse's back and landed in a small, muddy heap beside him, but damaged nothing. And then the door opened and Jonathan was silhouetted against the light, and Sarah knew she had never in all her life been so glad to see another living human being.

She had no recollection of going up the path towards him and being drawn under the shelter of the porch, with his hands holding her under the light so that he could see her more closely.

'Sarah—what on earth are you doing?'

'He's out there—King Cole—' she gasped, and the doctor peered through the darkness, shook his head in disbelief, and pulled her into the hall, unfastening the sodden khaki waterproof jacket round which rain had seeped at the collar and cuffs, in icy trickles inside her inadequate knitted sweater.

'The—the horse,' she repeated, through chattering teeth, as her gloves followed the jacket over a chair, and the doctor opened a door and led the way into a small, firelit study. 'I—I put the reins over the gatepost—'

'Good girl,' he told her, pushing a chair up to the fire—a large, leather chair, with velvet cushions. 'Sit here and tell me what happened. It's a funny sort of a night for a ride, I'd have thought—'

She told him, as quickly and accurately as possible, and he stood by the telephone on the desk, his eyes intent on her face, assessing the situation.

'And you say the lines are down between the village and the hospital?'

'Yes, and between Courtney Place and there, too. So I couldn't ring you.'

'I see. Let's try this line—it was all right an hour or so ago—Philip called in.'

'The roads are blocked by fallen trees, so I couldn't drive here,' she went on, 'and Charlie Nixon couldn't drive for help either, so he had to come on foot to us—'

At that moment the hospital answered, and

in a few well-chosen words Jonathan outlined the circumstances and decisions were taken.

'I see,' he told Sarah, going to the sideboard. 'Well, the hospital are sending out an ambulance, and the fire service and traffic police are going with them to get the road cleared, so stop worrying about Mrs. Nixon.'

'I am worried,' Sarah said, still shivering, although she could feel the heat of the flames warming her hands and face. 'They might be ages getting to her.'

Jonathan nodded. 'True. Let's hope she can hang on until they get there. Here, drink this down, and then we'll clean you up, and find some dry things, and I'll have a look at that cut.'

He knelt before her and began to rub her hands gently in his big, warm ones. For a few moments she remained passive, her head against his shoulder, his hands warming hers, and then she lifted her head and tried to smile at him.

'Better now?'

She nodded. 'I'm sorry. It—it's just that I'm so glad I got here, and that you were here—'

'I know. Sit there a minute and have your drink while I get King Cole under cover and rub him down—back in about five minutes. You can wash yourself at the small basin in the cloakroom, it's warm in there, but be careful with that cut—'

She drank down the amber liquid, and washed her filthy hands and face in the hall cloakroom, where Jonathan had left a clean white towel for her. She found a small comb on a shelf, and tugged it through her wet, tangled hair, then washed and dried it and put it back on the shelf, and went back to the fire. She pulled off her wet socks and laid them on the fender to dry, curling her toes up in the warmth, pleased that sensation had returned all over her, in spite of her general wetness.

'Did the horse scare you?' Jonathan stood in the doorway, his hair ruffled and wet. 'I've got a small place at the back,' he explained. 'It won't be the first time he's spent a night here. He's warm and dry, and got some oats.'

Sarah nodded her approval. 'No, he didn't scare me,' she told him, as he washed his hands at the sink and came back to her. 'I thought he would, in fact I was certain he would, but Melissa was right—he knew what to do, and he did it. What a marvellous animal he is, isn't he?'

Jonathan agreed. 'I'm going along to Mrs. Nixon, Sarah. There's a good chance I'll get through in the station-wagon, going by the village road. The rain is stopping, and the water should be going down on the roads. I'll probably be there before the ambulance. I might even deliver the baby—' He said this with such relish that Sarah shot a quick glance at his face, and found it lit up with anticipation, giving its powerful dark lines an astonishing charm.

'You'd like that. Wouldn't you?'

'I would, certainly. Wouldn't you?'

Sarah considered, or pretended to consider, knowing the answer. 'Yes, I'd like that, very much.'

Jonathan changed the subject.

'Now that you're warmer I'll find you some dry things. I expect they'll be a mixture of Philip's and his aunt's. I won't be a minute.'

The mixture consisted of a man's T-shirt, an Aran sweater and a pair of cord jeans, which weren't too bad when turned up at the bottoms.

'Where is Philip?' Sarah asked, more for something to say, and was told that an old man was dying in the next village, and the junior partner would probably be out all night.

'I see. By the way, Melissa knew I could ride. She guessed quite early on.'

Jonathan grinned at her, snapping his bag shut and coming over to the fire, where he stood looking down at her.

'I guessed,' he said. 'Why should you deceive her, any more than you deceived me, about the riding? That is one thing she really knows about. It became a game for her, I suppose. Listen, the kettle's boiling, I'll make some tea.'

'I don't want any tea, not after that whisky,' she said. 'But I want to come with you. You ought to go now—'

'I am going now,' he said.

'—but I want to talk to you, there's so much I have to tell you! Let me come with you, please, Jonathan. I promise I won't get in the way! Please—'

She got to her feet, and he pulled her to him and kissed her mouth gently.

'You really want to, don't you?'

'Yes, I do. I can cheer Charlie up, and tidy things away, and see to the children, if they're awake—all sorts of things. I'm quite good at it—'

He smiled. 'Oh, I know, Sarah ... I do know! All right, let's find you a waterproof coat, or something, and you can tell me all these things you are bottling up inside you as we go.'

She was surprised to see that only ten minutes or so had elapsed since her arrival—it seemed more like ten hours. The doctor insisted on looking at the small cut on her forehead, and cleaned it and put on a small sticking-plaster, and then they were once more out in the wild wet night, but this time Sarah felt quite safe and confident, beside Jonathan Lord in the big station wagon, the powerful engine surging beneath her as had King Cole's great muscles.

'You're a good lass,' he said, as he drove

carefully down the lane, peering through the windscreen. 'Why did you do it?'

'Do what? Come for you, do you mean? I told you it was Melissa's idea, really. But I suppose there were several reasons. I was worried about Mrs. Nixon . . . really worried. I knew you'd be furious if we didn't get a message through to you. It seemed the only thing to do, I suppose—'

She watched his hands on the wheel, strong and skilful, and very sure. 'And I had to prove to you that—' She broke off, at a loss for adequate words.

'That what?' His voice was very gentle.

'Prove something—I don't know, Jonathan. Prove that I cared, perhaps. You see, you've always thought I didn't care—since my dreadful mistake about Melissa's pony—'

There was a long pause.

'That's not correct, Sarah.'

'Yes, it is. You were furious with me that evening. I know you were—' Her voice trembled. 'I—I saw your face. I thought you would never forgive me for being so stupid—never.'

Jonathan sighed. 'Dear heaven, women!' he mused. 'Listen, love. You did no harm that night. Someone had to say "your pony" to Melissa one day, sooner or later, and it just happened to be you. It was a bit fraught, but she soon calmed down and went to sleep and that was it—it was over. And little harm done.'

Sarah stared ahead, unconvinced.

'You were angry—I know you were,' she said quietly. 'It made me feel awful, I wanted to give up nursing.'

He swore quietly to himself and took one hand from the wheel for a moment and found her hand.

'No, Sarah. Perhaps I was angry, but for another reason—'

'Another reason?'

He nodded. 'I was worried about you. I knew it was a shock for you, saying that, and seeing your patient react, and then—' he paused, his voice hardening as he remembered—'I saw you with Gresham. His arms round you, comforting you. That made me very angry.'

Sarah closed her eyes, her hands clasped tightly in her lap, her throat aching with tension.

'Or to put it another way,' he went on, 'I was very jealous. There you are, Sarah Vane. Satisfied?'

She let out her breath in a long, slow sigh, her heart pounding with delight.

'Philip means nothing to me any more,' she said softly, watching his profile. 'You don't know what really happened at the General. I left—ran away, because I thought I loved him and I wanted to marry him. When he said he had no plans for marriage I couldn't take it. But Philip let everyone think that I jilted him—he told me so, recently. The SNO there was mad with me—and quite rightly, too, as she doesn't go much for young nurses who "set their caps" at young doctors and then get disappointed. So Philip thought it would look better for me if he let people think I jilted him and not the other way round. That way I didn't look so stupid and pathetic. It was nice of him, wasn't it?'

To her amazement Jonathan was laughing.

'What's so funny?' she enquired coldly.

'I know all this,' he told her. 'I've known quite a long time.'

'About Philip and me, what really happened?'

'All of it.'

'How do you know?'

He laughed again. 'Medical, or hospital grapevine, love. The SNO in London knew about it. It seems her colleague at the General wasn't totally convinced by Philip's white lies in your defence. Your Miss Warden at St. Benedict's knew she had a somewhat heart-broken nurse coming to her, and kept you very busy and fully stretched, as therapy.'

Sarah shook her head. She recalled how hard the first few months at St. Ben's had been. How there had been no time for thought, let alone recreation. No time for brooding or self-pity. Everyone had known, it now seemed.

'It's awful,' she protested. 'I'd no idea.'

He grinned. 'You can't hide a lot from doctors and nurses, Sarah. Just as I found out about your grandmother, and why you had taken this post. I guessed that you wouldn't tell me yourself. Too proud, too stubborn, perhaps?'

Sarah pondered. Was she proud, even stubborn? She had certainly misjudged Dr. Lord, who knew so much about her...

Sarah sighed and curled up on the seat, and thought about the night's events, so far. It would be good to relax here and sleep, leaning against Jonathan's shoulder, but he had brought her along to help him, if she could, not to sleep.

As if he read her thoughts, he suddenly commanded: 'Talk to me, Sarah. I've got to drive slowly here, and we'll not be there for a few minutes. Tell me about you.'

'Me? I'm not very interesting, and I'm a fool, as you know.'

'You're not. And you are interesting to me.'

She frowned. All right, she thought. Two could play at the truth game, if that was what he wanted.

'I was jealous, too,' she offered.

'Of what?'

'Of whom,' she corrected primly. 'Of

Karen Ludvika.'

'Of Karen? How foolish! She has a tame brain surgeon waiting back there somewhere among all those fjords and lakes.'

Sarah raised her brows. 'You could have fooled me,' she snapped.

Jonathan shrugged. 'Well, she was available for company. You were there, but not available.' He paused to let this telling remark sink in. 'Karen is beautiful, but a creature with high morals. Are you pleased?'

She shrugged. 'And then there's Melissa's mother. I'm jealous of her, too.'

Jonathan sighed. 'June? Listen, Sarah. I'll be honest with you. We had something going, years ago, just after she left Paul Courtney. She's a difficult woman to say "no" to, when she wants something.'

'And she wanted you?'

'Maybe. Or just a stop-gap. Something to restore her confidence in herself as a woman.'

'Does she still want you?' So Melissa had been right, for all her youth and inexperience. Sarah knew her question was naïve in the extreme, but she had to know.

'I don't know, Sarah. I doubt it. Perhaps she just thinks she does. I'd like nothing better than to see June back here, with her daughter. But the danger is that it could make them all more unhappy than they are now. She has her music, her career, her public ... the bright lights she craved for.

Paul and Melissa have found some sort of peace without her, although it's been harder for the child.'

'Not such a child any more.'

'Indeed. In a year or so Melissa will be a woman. A miserable June, penned in there, playing at being little wife and mother, wouldn't do any of them any good. And Melissa would know—she's pretty perceptive.'

Sarah pondered over all this. He was probably right. As things were, Melissa loved and respected her mother, but would she still, if June came back and tried to act a part for which she was so ill-suited?

'And Paul—Mr. Courtney?'

Jonathan shrugged once more. 'Paul made his mistake when they married, and he knows it. He's a loner—wedded to the land, Sarah. He and June have a reasonable relationship now.'

She sat in silence, her thoughts whirling. Melissa, her parents, Philip and Evelyn, Gran and Michael at the cottage ... la Ludvika ... King Cole ...

'Wake up,' Jonathan told her, and she opened her eyes to find the station-wagon at a standstill, and him standing by her open door, holding out his hand.

'Come on, acting-unpaid-part-time midwife Vane ... we've arrived.'

CHAPTER SIX

Charlie Nixon opened the cottage door to them, his thin face pale and drawn, but with an excited gleam in his eyes.

'Ee, Dr. Lord, Sister said you'd come, if you could get through. And Miss Vane, nice to see you again, I'm sure. Come on in, both of you.'

He led the way up the narrow staircase to where, in the small, low-ceilinged room crowded with heavy old-fashioned furniture Elizabeth Nixon lay. She looked pale and tired, the dank hair plastered to her temples, her eyes wide and bright, but she gave them a big smile.

'They're on their way from the hospital,' Jonathan told her as he stripped off his waterproof and suit jacket, motioning to Sarah to follow suit. Evelyn Gresham appeared in the doorway, not looking at all surprised, and both Sarah and Jonathan saw that she had a man's white handkerchief wrapped round her right hand.

'Hurt yourself?' Jonathan enquired, as he stood with the patient's wrist in his hand.

'I tripped as I was on my way here,' the older nurse said. 'It's nothing.'

'Yes, it is, Doctor,' Elizabeth Nixon said quickly. 'It's a nasty gash. She did it clambering over that tree trunk.'

Jonathan gave a look in Sarah's direction which said it all, and she turned to Evelyn.

'Let's have a look at it, then, Sister,' she said. 'Where's the bathroom?'

Sarah ignored Evelyn Gresham's protest and washed the gashed hand and applied a sterile dressing, noticing that the older woman looked tired and worn.

'A cup of tea,' Sarah suggested. 'Let Charlie make it, and then go and have a sit down, Sister. Jonathan—Dr. Lord will call if he wants you, I know.'

'You going to lend a hand?' Evelyn asked, and Sarah said that she hoped so. Although she was not much more than a beginner.

When Evelyn had been persuaded to sit by the fire in the sitting-room Charlie took Sarah to the kitchen and they made tea and took Evelyn a cup, and she left Charlie alone at the bare scrubbed table, with his tea and thoughts.

'The patient is doing fine,' Jonathan told her, back in the bedroom, in Elizabeth's hearing, but on the landing he had told Sarah that if the ambulance could get her to the hospital in time they would probably deliver the baby by Caesarean section, as Elizabeth was already bleeding, and would soon need a tranfusion.

Sarah studied Jonathan's dark, intent face and gentle hands, and knew that if she ever had a child she wanted him to be there, with her.

'Put that gown and mask on,' Jonathan suddenly told her sharply, and something in his face made Sarah's heart miss a beat. Was the child going to be born there—a fearful risk, with the mother bleeding so much? Would the ambulance never come?

'You'll be all right,' she heard him tell the patient. 'Trust us, Elizabeth, and it'll be all right.' Sarah lost track of time as she did what she was told, some inborn instinct helping her to do the right thing, knowing that he was a joy to work with—an education and also an inspiration. It was as though Sarah had done it all before, all that she had read in books and seen on film and discussed with colleagues engaged on midwifery, and she smiled to herself with pure delight, her fatigue forgotten.

'Get Sister up here fast,' Jonathan said suddenly, and Sarah found to her surprise that Charlie Nixon was sitting out on the landing, ready to spring into action at any moment, and he leapt down the narrow stairs and Evelyn came hurrying up.

Sarah then knew that if the baby was born in the cottage it would be Evelyn's experienced old hands that would hold him or her, working on resuscitating the child while Jonathan dealt with the mother. Outside, the wind had dropped, and the only sounds in the small, crowded room were the doctor's quiet voice and the mother's controlled breathing.

'They're here,' Charlie said, from his post at the top of the stairs. 'I heard 'em. They've made it, Doctor.'

Jonathan did not glance up or waste his breath.

'About time,' he said shortly. 'Tell 'em to bring that blood up, very fast. Get her ready for it, Sarah. Come on, Elizabeth, you're doing fine, girl.'

Sarah quickly cleaned the area on the patient's skin, ready to receive the transfusion, and told her what they were going to do, and as the ambulance man carried the blood into the room it all happened.

'Here we go,' Jonathan Lord said; Elizabeth Nixon uttered a loud, triumphant cry, and the ambulance man stood in the doorway, transfixed.

'It's a girl,' Evelyn Gresham said. 'A lovely, lovely little girl, pet—' and Jonathan asked the ambulance man to lend Sarah a hand with the transfusion, which he did, delighted to be of use, and to show off his skills.

For a few moments there was anxiety about the baby's breathing, and the doctor and midwife bent over the tiny form trying to clear the air passages, until at last a thin angry cry filled the room, and they all smiled and looked at each other, and the mother said that she wanted to see her, that her name was Dawn, and could Charlie come in and see them?

'Didn't think we'd make it,' Jonathan said very quietly to Evelyn. 'They'd have done a section at the hospital.'

'I know,' she said triumphantly. 'But we weren't in the hospital, were we, and we made it—you made it, Doctor!'

Sarah confirmed this. 'You were great, both of you,' she enthused. 'All of you,' including the patient in her delight as the two nurses got her ready for the ambulance.

'Get the baby ready,' Jonathan told Evelyn and supervised the final departure from the bedroom, descending the staircase behind the stretcher and carrying the bottle of blood in his hand.

'Bob next door says his phone's come back on,' Charlie announced in the hall, his eyes glued on his new child as Evelyn carried her downstairs. 'And the ambulance is connected to the hospital by radio an' all.'

'So it is,' Jonathan said, watching as his patient was lifted aboard, followed by the midwife with the baby. 'Put me on to the hospital, will you?'

And for a few moments he spoke to his colleague over the air and gave details of what to prepare for. When he rejoined Sarah in the road he studied her face for a moment, and then turned to the ambulance.

'Give me Dawn, Sister,' he said briskly. 'Staff Nurse here is pining—she hasn't touched her yet.'

And to Sarah's utter delight the baby was put into her arms for all of ten seconds, and then removed. But it was long enough for her to savour the warm weight of the child, hold the soft bundle close to her and look down into the crumpled pink face. Dawn Nixon, she said softly.

And it was almost dawn. True, a grey, feeble, watery dawn, but quite unmistakable.

'Nice, isn't she?' As Jonathan spoke, Sarah handed the baby back and Jonathan took her arm and led her to the front door as the ambulance drove away towards the town.

Sarah sighed. 'Lovely. Absolutely wonderful,' and allowed herself to be taken inside into the warmth of the cottage.

As she climbed upstairs to put the bedroom to rights Sarah thought about the time, so long ago, it seemed now, when Jonathan had talked to her in his car about this impending birth, and his anxiety about it. And how she had decided that evening that she would like to study midwifery one day.

Would she, still? Now the future was a blank sheet, awaiting orders, decisions, and plans. And so much now depended on Jonathan himself.

'Come on, Sarah,' he called up the stairs.

'Let's be off, if you've finished up there. Charlie must be fed up with all this—let's leave him in peace.'

Before starting the car he studied her pale, smudged face and tumbled hair, and the shadows of fatigue like bruises under her eyes. Big, bright eyes, that met his with a clear, unquestioning gaze. For a moment she thought that he was going to kiss her, but the old man in the cottage next to the Nixons' had come to the gate and was watching them with great interest.

So, instead, he called out something, letting his voice slur into the local accent, and waved good-bye to the Nixon children who were at their sitting-room window—small round faces, eyes huge with interest and bewilderment. Another round of waving, this time from Sarah as well, that took in the old man next door, and they were off.

'What do you want to do now?' Sarah was foolish enough to ask, as Jonathan drove carefully along the village road and headed for the open country.

His sudden smile made the blood flood her cheeks, and he repeated her question with a wicked gleam in his eyes.

'What do I want to do now?'

She longed to put out her hand and touch his face, smooth back his dark hair and trace the outline of his mouth with her finger-tip.

'What I really want, Sarah, is to take you to

my home, and talk to you, and see that you get some food and sleep. But meanwhile my place is full of Greshams, both sleeping, I expect, unless Philip is still out, which I doubt. Tired, working Greshams, bless 'em both, but a darn nuisance at this moment, this morning, now. What d'you say, Sarah?'

She closed her eyes and leaned her head against his shoulder and made no reply. It was enough to feel through his clothes the strength that had overwhelmed and frightened her at first, and still did, if she let it. But she could not control the surge of shining pleasure that his words caused. She turned her face close against his shoulder, and nodded slightly, knowing that he would feel her signal, and know that there were no words to say what she felt.

For a while he drove in silence, and then Sarah lifted her head and gazed sleepily through the window.

'Where are we?'

'Almost at Courtney Place,' he told her. 'I have to take you back there. They will be wondering about you—' He sighed. A very small sigh, but Sarah's acutely aware senses picked it up.

'And your plans for the immediate future? I understood you were going to move on to another case soon, anyway.'

Sarah shrugged. 'I've a lot to think about.

I'm not needed here much more, am I? Not by Melissa.'

'Correct.'

'I should go back to St. Ben's, I suppose—'

She threw this perilous suggestion into the air, and it sank like a stone in a duck pond, barely leaving a ripple.

'Here we are.'

Jonathan Lord swung the big vehicle through the great wrought iron gates of Courtney Place, now standing open as if to greet them, and the water from the drenched ground rose in a cloud of spray under his turning tyres.

As they approached the house Sarah felt as if a lifetime had passed since Evelyn Gresham woke her from a deep sleep, saying that she was needed downstairs. Needed. Who needed her now? Not Melissa, not her grandmother, who was so much better. Dare she believe that Jonathan did? But did he really need anyone? Sometimes it seemed that he had been alone, functioning as an independent unit, for so long that it was sufficient for him. But then, what did she know of this strange man at her side? He constantly revealed new facets of his complex nature, many of them extremely contradictory. Who could know or understand Jonathan Lord? Many like him, many even loved him, she thought. But who understood him?

You do, she told herself fiercely. He's arrogant but compassionate, impatient but dedicated, self-opinionated but just. All those things, and yet his whole personality cannot be summed up so easily by six neat adjectives.

They pulled up in the drive, and Sarah was suddenly aware of her ill-fitting borrowed clothes, her face that had received only the swiftest of washes since her wild ride, and her hair which now hung in a heavy tangle on her shoulders.

Control, she thought. That was his secret. He could control his mind so perfectly, just as he could control a powerful horse or a hysterical patient, or a junior colleague, or a girl who loved him ... What chance did she have to breach this wall, if so many before her had failed?

There was no sound when they pushed open the great door and entered the hall, except for the grandfather clock ticking in the corner and the dying gale beyond the thick walls.

Sarah walked silently along to Melissa's door and stood listening, but there was no sound.

All was well.

She returned to the hall. Jonathan Lord stood watching her, his head on one side, his eyes veiled.

'Where shall we go? I'm in dire need of sustenance, and you look like a waif—a stray kitten, even.'

A stray kitten, indeed. Sarah pushed back

her hair, dropped her borrowed jacket on a hall chair and led the way to the kitchen.

She found bacon and eggs and tomatoes and a loaf and a pound of butter, and as she worked Jonathan filled the coffee percolator and began to cut bread for toast. Soon the delicious aroma filled the air, and he stood beside her and watched as Sarah filled two warm plates, put two knives and forks into his pocket, picked up the plates and indicated that he should follow with the tray of coffee things, buttered toast and marmalade.

She padded on her bootless feet to the long hall where the big leather settee stood in front of the still-glowing remains of last night's great fire, and indicated that they would eat from the low coffee table.

They sat side by side and ate and drank, saying little—anticipating each other's needs, the doctor rising once to stir the fire and throw fresh logs on to the hot ashes.

'Why not let it go out now?' Sarah asked sleepily. 'It's morning now, well and truly.'

'Meaning that it's time I went?' he enquired, amused.

Sarah flushed. 'I didn't mean that—well, perhaps I did—' She broke off, totally confused.

Jonathan pushed the coffee table with its empty plates and mugs back, and crossed his legs comfortably, leaning back against the velvet cushions. He held out one arm, and

Sarah found herself wriggling towards him a few inches. Not far, but far enough for her to lean back in his embrace, his hand, warm and heavy, curved down over her shoulder.

'We need to talk,' he told her, his eyes closed, his dark head deep in the green velvet. 'You and I have broken all records, I'd say, for misunderstandings, crossed wires, lack of reasonable communication.'

Sarah nodded. 'I know, but you're not the easiest person in the world to communicate with.'

'I'm sorry. But neither are you, Sarah.'

She digested this news in silence. He was probably right, although she had never thought about it before.

'You're very good professionally,' he went on, almost as if he could read her mind. 'But you retreat, Sarah. You hide behind that lovely face, and it's impossible to know what you're thinking.'

'Perhaps it's just as well, sometimes.'

'Maybe. But there have been many occasions when I would like to have known. I expect you've hated me quite a lot.'

She frowned. Hated him? Resented and even feared, but not hated.

'I resented you. But why do we have to go over all this, Jonathan? I'm tired, and—' She wanted to tell him that she had endured enough misery over the past weeks, without more.

He turned, and drew her close to him, forcing her to look up into his face.

'Why? Because it has to be told, my love. If we are going to be married, and we are, you know.'

Sarah collapsed against him, powerless against his superior strength, and he held her close, stroking her hair, talking softly. He gave her a small shake.

'Did you hear me, Sarah? Say something, even if it's only "all right, Jonathan".'

She stifled a wild desire to giggle. Was this how men proposed? Or was this just the way they proposed to girls like her, with offhand, almost insolent informality?

'All right, Jonathan,' she heard herself whisper, and he bent his head and found her lips, and she knew that there was not, and never would be, anything casual or offhand about his lovemaking. This was one of the many things he did superbly well, and it mattered not that he knew it, because it was all part of the man.

'Right,' he told her, straightening up and arranging her beside him, her hand in his. 'You resented me. Because I came down hard on you when you arrived?'

She nodded.

'Well, I've already apologised about that. I have a quite unreasonable thing about young nurses who look for private cases—for financial gain. And I thought you were one, until I found out about you.'

'You apologised that time after my riding lesson, so-called, when you made me gallop down into the park, and then you chatted me up, under the trees.'

He threw back his head and laughed, and Sarah grinned reluctantly.

'Chatted you up? What an expression!'

'Well, you did, didn't you? You said you didn't go in for doctor-nurse relationships, and you made me furious.'

'Poor Sarah. Yes, I admit I did provoke you, but you look very exciting when you're upset, and I gave way to temptation. I knew that day that I wanted you. You knew, too, didn't you?'

'I was very unhappy,' she said. 'But okay, yes, so you apologised then, about being overbearing, but it didn't help, because I was falling in love with you, and I thought you despised me.'

'Never, Sarah. I thought that perhaps you and Gresham might come together again, which made me wild. I felt you disliked me, perhaps with good reason, which didn't help—and then you began to make plans to leave.'

'And you said nothing,' she said. 'Even a few kind words would have helped—'

He shrugged. 'Probably. When will you marry me, Sarah?'

She laughed up at him. 'In such a hurry,

Doctor? Soon, if you like. When I leave here. Now I'm going to carry these things to the kitchen—it's time we went to bed. I'm tired, you must be, too.' But he showed no signs of undue fatigue, as he pulled her down to him and buried his face in her hair. The breakfast dishes forgotten, Sarah took the line of least resistance and closed her eyes.

'Are Elizabeth and the baby going to be all right?'

'I expect so—I hope so. But don't let's talk about them, love. Are we going to be all right, Sarah?'

She shook her head.

'I—I don't know, Jonathan.'

'Why not?'

Because I don't know if you love me, she cried out silently. All right, you want me, and like being with me, and it's not enough.

'Perhaps because you think I'm foolish...'

'Sometimes you are. You were, in the past. But then I am, too.'

'Not you, Jonathan.'

'Ah, yes, my love. One day I will tell you.'

'Tell me now—'

'No, not now. All right, I don't suffer fools gladly—my reputation dogs my footsteps, doesn't it? But I liked and admired your work from the start. The way you handled Melissa, your loyalty, your honesty—everything. As for foolishness, well, I will always be a complete and utter fool over you. I have never thought you any of the things you think of yourself, the bad things. I still don't really know if you love me, but don't go away from me, Sarah—ever.'

She opened her eyes and stared at him.

'Jonathan,' she said quietly. 'I don't know if you love me, either.'

'You don't? D'you mean to say you don't know? Did I forget—did I leave it out?'

She nodded, her eyes enormous.

'I love you, Sarah. I love you, Staff Nurse Vane, soon to be Mrs. Lord. Good grief! I love you so much. Will that do?'

'Yes, thank you,' she said. 'But then you always do everything so beautifully, don't you, Jonathan?'

Photoset, printed and bound in Great Britain by
REDWOOD PRESS LIMITED, Melksham, Wiltshire